CARAVAGGIO

For Vivienne

Acknowledgements

Of the many books I consulted, the reader might like to know of the following:

The best and most recent conventional biography is *Caravaggio: A Life* by Helen Langdon (Chatto and Windus).

M by Peter Robb (Bloomsbury) is a speculative biography, which suggests possible solutions to the many gaps in the known history of the painter's life. I have drawn on some of his suggestions, most especially his speculations about Caravaggio's fate, which I find persuasive.

There are many books of reproductions of his paintings. *Caravaggio* by Catherine Puglisi (Phaidon) contains a full list as well as attributions, lost works and also pictures by his contemporaries.

Although the reader should be warned that some of the pictures I have referred to in the text have been lost to Mafia, war and history.

Finally, my thanks to my agent David Godwin, for his encouragement and advice. To my editor Maria Rejt for her good sense and judgement. And to Richard Cohen, Olympic fencer, for correcting my rusty swordplay.

CARAVAGGIO

DISCARDED

Christopher Peachment

THOMAS DUNNE BOOKS
ST. MARTIN'S PRESS ✄ NEW YORK

THOMAS DUNNE BOOKS
An imprint of St. Martin's Press.

CARAVAGGIO. Copyright © 2002 by Christopher Peachment. All rights reserved. Printed in the United States of America. No part of this book may be used or reproduced in any manner whatsoever without written permission except in the case of brief quotations embodied in critical articles or reviews. For information, address St. Martin's Press, 175 Fifth Avenue, New York, N.Y. 10010.

www.stmartins.com

ISBN 0-312-31448-5

First published in Great Britain by Picador
An imprint of Pan Macmillan Ltd

First U.S. Edition: May 2003

10 9 8 7 6 5 4 3 2 1

The virtue of a historical novel is its vice –
the flatfooted affirmation of possibility as fact.

Anthony Burgess. *A Dead Man in Deptford*

Author's Note: There is an inaccuracy in the very first sentence of this book, and many more thereafter.

CARAVAGGIO FECI

Prologue

I, Caravaggio, did this.

As I lie here in this sodden bed, I can see a number of my smaller goods stacked in the corner but little else, for I cannot move with ease. What they have done with the rest of my things, and the three or four rolled-up paintings I had with me, I do not know. There was a 'St John' there that was worth something. The kindly friar with the foolish face comes in three or four times a day to wash me, and force some food between my lips. They are also trying herbs on me. A tincture of asafoetida and something even more bitter, perhaps fenugreek. Much good it does me. I can see my face in the piece of smoked glass in the corner and it is yellow and disfigured. My limbs have no strength and I sweat continually. The wound to my face is terrible. Four years I have been travelling, on the run from the papal courts in Rome, through Malta and Sicily, and then finally I have wound up in Naples, a place I hate, and which has nearly been my undoing.

I have moments when I am lucid, however, and this is one of them. If I were lettered I would set it all down. But I am not, and anyway my story is all there in my paintings.

All there, if only you have eyes to see. I have carried a few of them with me, as testament to my life and what I have done with it. Read them, as you would read a book, and you will see. For I did this.

I am a proud man, and used to being so. I walked the earth on my two feet. I dressed in black, only the finest suits of princely velvet made by the best of tailors, and I wore them one at a time until they were rags, and then I spent my last *scudi* on another fine set. And now I am reduced to this. Just thinking of it makes the old anger rise again in my throat. The rage that once gave meaning to my life is still there, but it is weak. It warms my veins only a little. If only I could . . . But no, now there is nothing but a cold fever and sweat, fever and sweat.

When I was younger my rage would have me in its grip and nothing, *nothing* but hate would govern me. It made me arch my back like a cat, and my very head would smoke with the passion of it. Oh, the things it made me do. Things that would turn your stomach, things that would frighten you to an early death, things that made me feel like a god. And now I can barely raise an arm. That it should come to this!

They sent me a confessor. A gaunt man. I could not tell his age for he hid his head in his cowl and wrapped his bony hands in his robes. But his voice was mild and soft. He did not use the usual words. He just bid me tell the truth. That made me suspicious, I can tell you. In Sicily, where I was not long ago, they say that there are three kinds of truth. The truth you tell the tax collector. The truth you tell to God. And then the truth so terrible that you keep it to yourself entire. I know only the last kind.

But I mumbled something to him, something about a brawl in Rome and a death they said I caused. And my whoring, of course. They always like that one. Everyone confesses to that one, in a whisper, which suggests that at last they are speaking true and that they fear damnation. The priests like that one too, because it makes them feel superior, never having tasted a woman, and it gives them a rise. And then they can absolve you so easily, and make themselves God-like too. I know priests. They are no different from the rest of us. And I know you. I look into your eyes, and I know you all, only too well. Because I know myself. And I do not fear damnation. Far from it, I welcome it. All my life I have lived without hope, and without fear.

But I did more, much more. And worse. There were two murders, that much I know at least. Perhaps there were more. I neither know, nor – and here is the part that fills, my weak body with a faint glory again – nor do I care. To murder a man is nothing. What of it? A brief ecstasy, a brief satisfaction of my itch, and then nothing more than the sadness that washes over you after coupling. And then the growing desire for more. There was drinking and brawling and whoring and sodomy. I could see my confessor's eyes flicker slightly at the mention of that last.

Ah yes, sodomy. The pleasure of the damned. In Milan, where I was raised and where I learned my craft, it was an affectation for the aristocracy. They fooled with it, as a child toys with a plaything. But not me. There was no fooling in me, I gloried in it. When my blood was up there was no other remedy but a man, taken roughly, where he stood and it was then that I felt most truly myself. I could have been hanged for it, but I did not care. In fact that very thought increased my pleasure a hundredfold, the thought that they might discover us and drag us away in ignominy to a cell with the Jews and whores and heretics. Oh, the peril of it, and the delight. And then there was theft and mayhem and rape and spying and much, much more that I enjoyed beyond all measure.

I, Michelangelo Merisi, known as Caravaggio, did this.

If I tell you my story crudely, you must forgive me. You cannot trust a murderer to have a fancy prose style.

To Begin

The painter should be solitary . . .

Leonardo da Vinci. *The Book of Painting*

Of my parents I will say little. God knows there is little enough to say. My father was in service to a local duke, a high-born one as a matter of fact, and so one for whom I had some time. My father called himself an architect and it was true he could draw up plans and oversee the making of small buildings or additions to buildings. He was a skilful mason, but the duke required him to be a steward, and so that was what he did for the most part. My mother did little but raise my brothers. A strange woman, for she often declared to us and to others that her marriage was unhappy, yet she continued in it like any other marriage, and did not seem so very distressed. I could never entirely understand them. The reason for this, I think, was that I realized at a very early age that I was cleverer than the both of them together. And that set me at an angle to the world.

When I was six I did a small sketch of the building next to ours. I had been drawing in secret for as long as I could remember. And my mother found the scrap of paper with my drawing and took it later to my father and from the next room I could hear them wondering aloud. And my father became cross, thinking I must have strayed and taken lessons from a stranger or a better architect than he. It was then I knew I had something that no other person had, although I could not put a name to it, being too young. And I would look at my parents from then on in a wholly new light. They were stupid. And I was not.

I think that most children have cause at some time or other to think that they are not the true offspring of their parents but foundlings who were taken in. Not surprisingly, it is a thought given mainly to the lower orders, who vainly dream of a better station in life. No prince ever thought to disown his parentage. But me, I knew that feeling most acutely. Not for any reasons of envy for a higher station. But because of my intellect. For how can it be that two stupid people can give birth to a child more intelligent than they? Surely, nature would not countenance such a monstrous oddity.

And I am monstrous, I know it. I had an eye for drawing but it began in odd ways that even now I cannot entirely understand. For I could not see the world then as I later found it to be. It may be that I had something awry with my sight, or some contortion of the brain, I do not know. But, when dark had descended and the place was full of shadows, I would often be startled by phantoms and ugly things, which minutes later I could not find. The foolish and the ignorant in the outer-lying regions are much taken with superstitions and fancy that they see fairies and spirits and such. I saw similar, but could not put a name to them, nor, being young and unknowing, could I compare them with other things.

But see them I did, and can remember their shapes still. Horned things, and creatures that could fly without wings, and near-humans of terrifying ugliness. They never frightened me. And as I grew older they came to me less and less. By the time I was six years old they had all but gone. Which is why I took to scrawling pictures on scraps of cloth and paper, to try to bring them back.

I never wanted my parents to see those drawings, and so I would always destroy them after by tearing them up and throwing them in the privy, or defacing them in some way.

I said I was monstrous and it is true. There were mirrors in our house, for we were not poor. But strangely I never believed what I saw in them. What the glass shows me is a swarthy man, not handsome, but not repulsive either, with large eyes, a fleshy nose and full lips. My hair is black and unruly, and my beard sparse. There is something of the Moor in me, some ancient blood unknown in my parentage. My friend Minitti sketched me thus, and that is what is in the glass, true enough. But it is not how I see myself.

From an early age I would look at my reflection in a large

copper pot that was kept polished in the kitchen. And also in the backs of silver spoons that belonged in the duke's palace. And what I saw there, I believed. A bladder-faced monster with squinting eyes, huge carbuncular nose and a hideous thick-lipped mouth twice as big as any other person's and liable to gobble down his neighbour just to fill it. No matter that the glass said otherwise. What you believe is more important than what is.

Do other children scare themselves in such fashion? I do not know. Perhaps they do. You will be saying to yourself at this point 'yes' or 'no', for you will recall not just your own childhood but that of others too, and will have talked to others of their childhood and will know all sorts of things about that general state. But I do not know. I had no childhood like any other. I hated being a child. I did not like being smaller than adults, for I could see more clearly than most of them, yet I was at their mercy because of my size. And so my chief memory of childhood is of waiting. Waiting for the tiresome state to pass. Waiting to grow to my full stature, and take my place in the world. Nor did I involve myself with other children. I despised them. I had no taste for their games. And I knew I was different.

Often I would look at my parents, and indeed at my uncle and his wife and at other married couples, and wonder why people got married. It is surely not for reasons of happiness, for I never saw one marriage that ever gave both parties happiness. Nor can it be for reasons of children.

Most parents love their offspring from duty and fear, not for what they are. Nor can it be for sexual relief. It is always cheaper to get that from a whore. The price you pay, eventually, is lower than the price you pay for a wife.

As to having children . . . I would sooner hack my balls and clacker off and live celibate than even entertain that idea.

One night my uncle died. Then my grandfather and then my father, all in the same night, all of the plague. All I remember is being the object of much pity, and being held a lot and kissed and caressed, which I did not like. Otherwise I was glad to be rid of them. They were a smelly lot.

I did not play with my brothers, did not even have much to do with them, bar what could not be avoided around the house; and at thirteen, my mother was relieved to see me go. I should have tarried a little longer, only so that I could secure a better position than I did, but impatience marks my life, and even at thirteen I was so marked.

Peterzano, known as Simone, had no great claims to genius, although that did not stop him making them. He told people he had been a pupil of Titian, and that claim much impressed the credulous, so that he got commissions for portraits that were clearly beyond his measure. He may well have met Titian at some point, perhaps sat at his feet and ground up some of his pigments. Perhaps even filled in some background detail of the man's work, I do not know. But I doubt he was a pupil, for his works are so far behind the master he can have learnt nothing. But I did not know that much of art at thirteen. And he was kind to me.

He took me in, and gave me food and a roof for four years and taught me all he knew, which God knows was not greatness, but was a good enough grounding. And indeed, truth to tell, I am grateful he was not a master. For I knew I would find my own style, and I knew that I would find it sooner if it was not clouded by another's. He was perhaps the sort of teacher all painters who aspire to greatness should have. A dogged craftsman who can teach you everything but that final thing. What that final thing might be I cannot name, but I know it when I see it. And of recent painters, only Titian will I acknowledge as having it.

Having it? I am sorry, I am wrong on that score. It had him, and it had him in spades. He was possessed by it, and it worked through him and shone like a burning tree in the desert night. I speak here unusually, I know, and not quite clearly. I wish I were a lettered man. But this is the only way I can describe it to you. I have known that state. And believe me: it possesses you. You toil and you toil and you labour even longer and nothing will come right and then suddenly, you will do a small stroke, without any thought behind it, and there it is. You will step back and wonder at it, for just suddenly, just so, there is perfection. And you know not where it came from.

Others, I know, work differently, but that is how it is for me. Some men, cultured men, men who are collectors and

12

patrons, have a name for it; which I will not use here. I am more careful. And I do know this. It may come of its own accord. But it will not come unless you sweat hard first. You cannot make it happen just by sitting around and hoping for it to happen. Nothing comes of nothing. First you must sweat.

Where was I . . . ah yes, Peterzano. What more can I say of him, I have already filled as much space as he deserves. Posterity will find him a good enough hack. And wonder where on earth I got my mastery from. Stay with me, and I will try and tell you.

Four years I stayed with him in Milan. And I worked hard and justified the money my parents had given him for my apprenticeship. And at night I would slip from the window to my room, and roam the streets in search of forbidden pleasure.

The aristocrats of Milan toyed with male love. It was not a serious pursuit for them, but it was like a secret fashion, and one which had to be affected, if they were to be thought refined. I did not hawk myself, like so many of the pretty young men hanging around their fashionable places. I am not pretty, and I have nothing of the feminine about me, and so have no taste for kissing; nor will I suck another man; nor let him into me. But if you want it up the arse, then I am your man.

Besides, Milan was ruled by the Spanish in those days. And a Spaniard will fuck anything with a heartbeat.

As I will tell you, the penalties for sodomy were extreme. But if you made sure you only fucked the high-born, then you were moderately well protected. No ordinary policeman was going to drag a duke or a cardinal from his salon and throw him in jail with a bunch of Jew moneylenders; not unless he wanted a dozen lawyers howling down on his arse and getting him thrown out of his job. No, the police stuck to chasing the lower orders; and so I stuck to fucking the upper. You know where you are with nobility.

Besides I knew that if I was going to make my way in the world as a painter I was going to need a patron, and that meant a patron who had connections as much as money. I need very little money in this life. Material goods hold little value for me. But I knew even at an early age that I was going to need all the protection I could get. And since I do not have a taste for friendship, then I would need to forge the bonds with a protector by other means. Sex seemed as good a way as any.

So I fucked the prettier ones and I even fucked the ugly ones, for when they are turned away from you, what is the difference? Besides, the ugly ones were so grateful. And I fucked women too, even though I sometimes paid for it. They feel different, and it is often more soft and more pleasant and sweet with a woman. But it lacks that element of danger. And sex without danger is like meat without salt.

I did not care for Milan. A large city, but an unhappy one, with grey skies and little by way of good building. I did not like the Spanish rulers, a stupid, vain and cruel bunch, who strutted around proclaiming their superiority. I do not mind arrogance, especially if it is justified. *Sprezzatura* is becoming in a man, but only if he has earned it. The Spanish think they can affect airs without having made the slightest justification for them. They lack cunning too and so will never be good rulers. They cannot placate or flatter their subjects and so the people under them will become sullen and prone to revolt. And the Spanish like to put down dissent with steel and fire. They will never be loved, only feared. Every race in the world has some good reason to hate the Spanish. I have seen it all too often.

Milan was a town of arms and armourers. Some of the finest suits of armour in the land were made in Milan. Princes came here for their fancy hand-tooled suits of armour which were only ever going to be shown off in some parade of vanity. But then there were the serious armour-makers. These men knew something of war and they designed their armour most carefully, with angles and rounded edges and special curves, which were so fashioned as to deflect an arrow's flight, or make a sword glance off it. They were masterpieces and lovely to look at in their way.

I saw a landsknecht once, a huge, bearded Switzer, whose arms were covered in scars and open gashes. He was ordering a cuirass for his mighty chest from one of the smaller armourers and he took great pleasure in discussing its shape and where the curves should go, just so, and just so. And he demonstrated to the smith how the piece was to be hammered and what thicknesses it should have and where. And he showed the man how sword thrusts came at a soldier and which were the deadly ones and which were the harmless ones, and how they were best parried or deflected or ignored.

He would adopt a stance, whether the defensive or the offensive, and he would twist his body to show how his armour should take a blow. And how the area where the arm joins the body is most vulnerable, because it must be mobile and so unprotected, and how there is an artery in there which if cut can let a man bleed to death in minutes. And how he therefore used chain mail to cover that spot, even though it chafed and a light foot soldier could still sneak a dagger in though the gaps. You could only minimize the risks, never eliminate them. Besides he was a soldier. And the minute a soldier begins to worry about risk, then he had best go home.

I sat in the shadows in the corners and listened for a whole afternoon without noticing the time, so taken up was I. And I pondered on a soldier's life. It had its attractions; but not for me. I had my own colours calling me home.

The main thing that Peterzano had me do was grind his colours. I could already draw better than he, and anyway I had lost the taste for it. He was supposed to teach me fresco work too, and sure enough I mastered it quite quickly, but, as I will explain to you later, I found it tiresome and gave it up, only to try it once in my life, with nearly fatal consequences. Fresco colours are pathetic, all milky and anaemic. Oil colours were what I liked and they alone would be my mistress. The ochre and the cerulean and the rest.

Arms and Armour

The painter should be solitary and consider what he sees . . .

Leonardo da Vinci. *Book of Painting*

The other thing I learnt in Milan was how to fight. I told you that Milan was a city of armourers and it was true, and they also made good swords there too. Not as great as they say Toledo in Spain could manage, but many Spanish blade-makers came to Milan to pursue their trade and it was said to be the best outside of Spain. Most of the smithies could hot-forge a blade in a morning and have it back with the armourer to have the handle and guard fitted and the blade decorated with engravings by the afternoon. But one man there was, who they said had studied in the East, and had learned the secrets of the Japanese swordsmen, and his blades were much sought after. He used to hammer them cold, which took much strength, and aid from several assistants. He was much admired as a *ferraro*, or smith.

He would hammer the blade out to one and a half times its proper width then fold the blade back in on itself to its true width and then hammer it out again to one and a half again, then fold it back, and so on, hammering each fold perhaps twenty or twenty-five times until he was satisfied with the strength of the blade. Then he would take it to a sharpener who would give it an edge. And then he would test it.

He kept an old iron cannon in his yard, and he would test each sword on it. He would run at the cannon uttering strange foreign cries, quacking like a duck, and grunting as the apes do, then swing at the cannon with his new sword, and, damn me, a great hunk of iron would flake off the muzzle of the gun, with a sound like ten bells falling from a spire; and the man would hack and hack away until the gun had lost several inches of skin, and then he would inspect the blade, and if it had kept its edge, only then would he sell it. He was a strange man, but he sold a lot of swords.

I went to him once when I had some money. And I spoke to him as I had heard others speak to him on swords, and let him think I might be a soldier. And he indulged me. He took from the wall a sword and handed it to me, and even as I took it and hefted it, I betrayed myself as no sort of soldier and he laughed at me, but in a kindly fashion.

And so he taught me a little, since every man should know how to bear arms, he said, even if he was not a soldier. For if you learn to bear arms then you will also lean how to bear yourself. Always walk, he said, as if you carried a sword. Walk like an armed man and few will attack you, no matter if they outnumber you or you plainly have no sword. Keep up a front, he said, and the world will respect you and keep a respectful distance. I liked that idea. And carried a sword for a while even though it was strictly illegal. A sword does something for a man. It gives him mettle. Or what I later heard an Englishman call 'bottom'.

And so he taught me more. He taught me the main moves of fencing. He taught me the on guard position and the thrust and the parry. And he taught me the quarters of the body from *prime* to *septime*, *seconde* to *octave*. And he was a very good teacher, for he could see that I would not ever become a soldier and so did not have to work long and hard at my fighting technique. What he saw in me was that I would need, at divers times, a means of protection, and so he taught me the sound rudiments and then just enough practice for me to get by. 'For you will not be called on to duel, Michelangelo,' he said, 'duelling is for knights and the high-born, and not for the likes of you.'

Mark, he said it kindly; but, O God help me, I felt myself colour and the blood slowly crept up my face and I did not know what to do, for already I was trying to stammer my thanks, and say, 'Think nothing of it,' but then my blood was up and my ears were pounding with it as if a squadron of cavalry were cantering through my head, and oh by Christ I could not restrain myself but took the sword and swung it at him.

Thank God he was a master. He was startled, but never

lost his nerve for a moment. The stool came up in one swift motion, caught my blade and turned it away, and then from nowhere his dagger was at my throat and I was panting heavily, but my blood was still up and my eyes stung. My tongue was bloated and stuck in my mouth because it was so dry, but I cursed and swore at him that if I was not of high enough standing for him then he had best strike me down now where I stood, or else I would come after him and kill him for the insult.

And he stood and he stood, with blade at my throat and, God bless the man, he slowed me down, I know not how. He was breathing very easily and somehow, by some trick I think, he caused my breathing to align with his own and slowly I felt the blood drain from my head and then I began to sag. And he caught me with his arm about my waist and lowered me onto a chair where I slumped against the table. And he went for a cloth and some cool water and bathed my temples and began to talk to me, most softly and kindly like a nurse with a child, but never scolding.

This was the first and last time that anyone reacted so kindly to my rage. Other men have seen my temper, and they either run in fear from it, or else they chide me and bid me keep better control of myself. But I cannot. And this man alone knew it and saw it for what it was and took me at my face value. No man has ever done that for me before. And he won a place in my . . . I was about to say he won a place in my heart.

How easy it is to fall into a common lie when telling a story. No one wins a place in my heart. I have not got one.

Still, let me put it this way. There are very few kindnesses in this world. What passes for a kindness is usually done for a reason, whether for future gain, or advancement, or to ingratiate or to store up indulgences in heaven or for a hundred other base reasons. I am not even sure that this man knew he had done a kindness. He was a bluff, sturdy man, and a former soldier, not given to nicety or fancy manners. Yet he had shown me more understanding than any man I have ever dealt with. It should have improved me. But it did not, for his kind are as rare as snow in a summer valley.

And now that I was calmed, he laughed again, so gently, and said that with a temper like mine I had better learn about in-fighting than about fancy duelling, for I would more likely be found in a tavern brawl than a duel at dawn by some misty lake. So he taught me in-fighting. How a cloak may be used as a misleading device, to make your opponent think your body is in a different place than where it is, just as the bull-fighters in Spain do, so he said.

And the different thrusts and parries. And how there is no magic, all-powerful thrust that is known only to a few cognoscenti. Any thrust is capable of being parried. And if a man is a reasonably competent swordsman there is no reason why he cannot defend himself against the best in the world, except fate. For what will always intervene is the bitch fate. It is only a matter of time before any sword fighter makes a mistake. And what marks the true aficionado up from the merely talented is that he will be ready and trained to put his opponent's mistake to good advantage. And run him through and kill him. Duelling is not a sport. It is a matter of death.

Thrust and parry, thrust and parry, *septime* and *octave*, *prime* and *seconde*, keep the line at all times, keep the line or you die.

And how a cloak can have lead weights sewn into its hem, and it can be swung like a weapon and catch the other man full in the face and temporarily blind him. And how it can be rolled about the arm and used as a shield to parry and absorb another's sword, though this must be done most carefully, for a sword cut can be taken on an angle across the forearm with little damage done, but you must be very wary of a full thrust for that might pierce through to God knows what that lies inside.

I have seen the anatomists flay a body and probe the internal organs, and know what damage can be done once steel gets too deep inside.

And then he was so kind, he taught me a move that he had shown only to perhaps three or four others, those being men who could pay him handsomely for this trick. It was a set of complicated thrusts, but these he told me were just a preliminary to please the rich into thinking they were getting their money's worth. The main business was a feint at the lower belly, beneath the heart. Followed by . . . the very briefest hesitation. And here you have to be something of an actor. The hesitation must be entirely believable. No good signalling it, or muttering under your breath, it must arrive as if completely unintended. And if your enemy believes in your hesitation entirely, then there is only one possible move for him: he will parry *septime*. And if your hesitation was sincere, then you can disengage into the high line, and your blade is pointed just on the right shoulder.

From there you may please yourself as to your target. Run him through his shoulder for a nasty wound. Under the arm if you wish him to bleed to death. Or through the neck if you wish to make a point to the onlookers. Either way, he is then no more than a side of meat.

And after some weeks of talking with the armourer and learning much from him, he gave me a dagger. It was a lovely piece of work, with a handle made of smooth horn, and a small, scrolled hilt, and a good blade, well balanced with the fulcrum point at one third the way along the blade. So I could heft it easily and throw it with the sure knowledge of where its point would land. And it was very pleasing to have in my palm. And I vowed never to be without it, not even when I was asleep.

And I took it to an engraver, one that I knew near the main station, and had him carve these words upon the blade:

Nec Spe. Nec Metu.

No Hope. No Fear.

I had heard them or seen them somewhere, I know not where, but they struck me at the time as fine words, and they stuck with me as a good saying. When I gain a knighthood they shall be my family motto.

And I will, believe me I will. I will carve a path through men until the whole world lies dead about my feet, if a knighthood is at the end of it. Even though there be no one left alive to acknowledge it, I care not. I never cared for others' good opinions.

But if I do not care for good opinion, what need have I then for a knighthood? I cannot answer that question. All I know is that I will have one. For myself, if no one else. For myself alone, then.

And since it will not be by feat of arms, then I had better get good at something else.

That man who taught me to fight, and understood me so well, is dead now. His name was Daponte, and many called him Uncle Dap.

Venetian Evenings

The painter should be solitary and consider what
he sees and speak with himself . . .

Leonardo da Vinci. *Book of Painting*

When I turned eighteen, I left Milan in a hurry. The town
was becoming a little warm for me. Not that I had done half
the things they said I had done. But I had done some of
them. And I had done other things, which had not come to
light, and were best left so. A piece of advice: killing a man is
best done at dead of night where there is no witness. To do
it in a *campo* in broad day is asking for trouble. And when I
get bored, trouble is what I ask for.

Venice was Venice. What can I say about it that you do
not already know? I knew what she would look like before
I got there, and I was not wrong. Nor was I disappointed.
No doubt you too can see the place, even though you have
never been there. In bright light it is clean and the waters
sparkle in such a way as pleases the young and the besotted.
In the dark and rain it comes alive, the rain tending to soften
the city's harsher features and drive its people indoors. Which

is as well, for they are not a handsome race. There is just a suspicion of sweet rot about the place that appealed to me, as if it were a man with the gangrene, at the moment just before his dissolution and dying. Otherwise no surprises.

First I found lodgings in the poorer part, up near the Ghetto, where they put the Jews by law and charged them healthy rents and a good thing too. Jews are like bookmakers, I have yet to see a poor one. And for my first trip I went to the Salute. It hadn't been built yet, but never mind that, for on the ceiling of the sacristy there are some of Titian's scenes from the Old Testament, including a 'David and Goliath' that I liked very much. Except that Goliath is always portrayed as unfeasibly large, I do not know why. He used a strange, exaggerated foreshortening on the paintings, so that they only look right and true from a certain position on the ground. Move a span left or right and they become odd. But his colouring is what matters most to me.

I asked around about Titian and they said that he had died but ten years since, at a very old age, just after completing a *Flaying of Marsyas*. And I asked who his master was and they told me Giorgione, a man I remember Peterzano telling me of. And so I sought out Giorgione's paintings and what a marvel they were. There was one, which no one knew what to call, for it represented no scene that anyone could recognize, neither from the Bible nor from ancient myth. In it, a woman sits on a grassy bank, feeding her infant, while a soldier looks on, idly leaning on his spear. In spite of the clear light, there is a streak of lightning in the cloud and a storm is threatening in the background.

It is not much valued, because of its obscurity of meaning, but I think it masterly, for the man has painted nothing but what nature has presented before his gaze. There is nothing mannered nor overheated about its style, but rather a limpid, clear vision such as in the purest spring water. His colours are plain and unsullied, both sweet and pure, with tempered shadows, and he has no taste for drawing. Whether that be a careful decision or an unconsidered one I do not know. But I care not for drawing first either. It wastes time, and anyway I do not need to. Giorgione worked from what was directly in front of him, and so shall I. And if that insults convention, then the conventions will just have to swallow it. Or change.

It does also fly in the face of Peterzano's teachings. Good.

I shall work *alla prima*, straight to canvas.

Besides, they told me that while Titian learned from Giorgione, Giorgione in his turn learned from Leonardo. That is good enough for me. It is like the Apostolic succession. In just three degrees of lineage, I am connected to the great master of them all. And a great writer on the art of painting also. I did not read his book until I had joined Cardinal del Monte and was already established, but I wish I had done so. It would have saved me much time and grief.

My second trip was to the Arsenale, where they build the ships on which Venice's fortune so much depends. I could see the speed of it all. Here were hundreds of men, all working away like ants in an anthill, hammering away with saws and adzes and ropes and stuff, I know not what. They say they can put together a whole ship in less than a day. Since I do not know how long anybody else takes, I am not impressed. They can throw a dozen together over breakfast for all I care, you still won't persuade me to get onto one. As soon put yourself in prison, then dunk your head in a barrel of water until you drown. Nasty things, boats.

My third excursion was to the Zattere, where I saw Pound, walking in silence and not talking to anyone.

My fourth outing was to a glassworks, on the Dorsoduro. It caught fire and threatened to burn down the whole area, so they passed a law banishing all glassworks to the outlying islands such as Murano.

So I went to Murano. It was dull as shit. I didn't burn down the new glassworks though. I wasn't in the mood.

My fifth walk took me out in the rain.

My sixth, I went to Frari, there to see Titian's *Assumption*. Words fail me. It is the best brushwork that mortal man can achieve. I now have only two choices. Either give up painting, since there is little likelihood that I will ever match it. Or else I must surpass it. I pondered on this for all of two hours.

I will surpass it. Nothing can stop me now. And I lied, it was all of two seconds.

After that I wanted to leave Venice. But events took me over.

This place is too tightly run. The police are everywhere and have too close a grip on the population, much more than in Milan. And every one of your neighbours is an informer, running to the police and tattling about how your clothes were too sumptuous or how you owed them rent money or how you went to a whore. Dear God, they could do with seeing Milan and its ways.

The food is terrible. They fry liver, which tastes to me like an old tart's tongue after a night spent sucking off a crew of galley slaves.

There were things I liked, though. Walk into St Mark's Square after dark, when it is lit by rows of little torches, high up near the top storey, and the place is deserted, and the air is crisp and just a little clouded from the mists that rise from the canals, then you will see as great a vision as was ever dreamed up by the human imagination.

Also, the whores are the best in the country, which is only to say the best in all of Europe. They will wear a mask if you pay them, which makes them look sinister. One mask, which had a long hooked nose and a chin which rose to meet it, like a crazy person from the commedia, was like the visions I sometimes had as a child. And another whore, a fair-haired one with lovely thick thighs, showed me her body, which was entirely shaved of its hair; armpits, belly, arse and all. She looked like a child's puppet. She said that this was done after the fashion of Moorish women, from whom she had learned the art. And that she was much in demand among those priests who have the young in their care.

It is always good to have confirmation that priests are hypocrites. I have always known it, all along. You can confess anything you like to them, from stealing to murder, and will only get a bored 'Twelve Hail Marys,' in return. Confess to a quick rub with your mate or a fumble with a whore under the table, and then listen to the heavy breathing behind the screen and the demand for more details.

You cannot blame them I suppose, for celibacy in this world of temptation is too much to demand of mortal man. God gave us this strange equipment to enjoy, why then deny it? And he gave us pleasure, and that which pleases is good. I don't know when all this celibacy for the priests started. But nowhere is it in the Bible. And nowhere in Christ's teachings can I find one single word that he spoke on the subject of sex, if you discount the woman taken in adultery, whom he saved from stoning. So why this Church's obsession with our sex lives.

I do not understand it, but I suspect that if you control a man's sex life, then you control a very large part of the man indeed, and the Church these days is very much interested in having control. Convince a man that eating is sinful, and you will be amazed at the reduction in the population. Does that sound fantastical? Then substitute 'sex' for 'eating'.

They are not so very different, both being natural appetites. I will say no more on the subject. I am no philosopher, unlike my new friend Giordano Bruno.

Bruno I found near the Basilica, in the Piazza San Marco. He was a funny little thing, small but not ill-shaped, and fiery. He was preaching, as indeed were many others, and he had drawn a large crowd because he had an edge over the others. I did not understand a word he was saying at first, but saw that he was a good preacher for he had charisma, as if the Lord had blessed him with the gift of tongues, of which I have read.

He was ranting and banging on, fit to bust, so I stood at the back, scribbling his likeness on a piece of litter I had picked up. I said I do not draw before paintings, but I do it at other times, just for the practice, and to amaze people. I do not need to do it as an aide-memoire. I can remember every scene I ever saw, and every painting, as if it were branded onto my brain with a hot iron. But to give a man a brief likeness of himself always pleases him, especially when he did not know you were doing it, and so did not put on airs for the pose. You had best flatter them, though. I made Bruno a bit taller and broader than he was. With kinder eyes.

His eyes were too quick to be called kind. And he debated everything. Nothing went past him that he would not argue. I found it tiresome, not being an intellectual, but still I liked the man. There was something comical about him, as there always is about the very learned.

As to what he was going on about, neither I, nor many of the crowd so far as I could see, could make head or tail of it. There was much stuff about all the heavens above being mirrored here below on earth, which sounds perilously like a heresy to me. Not that I know much of the finer points of theology, but I do know that the Jesuits will argue anything they want up into a heresy, if they take against it. And the Jesuits take against most things, believe me. Watch what you say around one of that lot. Or your head will decorate a spike like a melon in the market.

Bruno was living close by the English Ambassador; a typical diplomat, he had a false dignity, which he stood on, and an ability to be loquacious on any topic under the sun except one of any importance. He could name the time to the nearest minute of his last good meal at Harry's bar but ask him what the Papal legate had said to him yesterday and he would bluster, lay on the charm and change the subject. And Bruno was so often in and out of the man's offices, I began to think he had some diplomatic business there.

And he did, after his fashion. When he had finished preaching one day, I waited for the crowd to disperse and offered to take him to a tavern, nearby. We sat on red velvet benches, and he took to me, I could see it. Not many men do that, for I am not so personable. Still, he had some depth to his perception, and was not taken in by an easy appearance.

And we talked. Or rather, he talked most, and I listened, interjecting only the gruffest of phrases and words of assent, for in spite of not understanding much of what he was saying, yet he had a strange effect upon me. Such that I found myself feeling drowsy, yet light-headed at the same time, and far from falling into a sleep, feeling more as if I were dreaming a very real sort of dream, while being very sure of being awake. There is no word I know of for this state. But I have seen surgeons bring it on with drugs and herbs before they cut into their patient. What they did with drugs, Bruno did with his voice.

And when he had finished he poked me in the ribs and pinched my cheeks and beamed at me and said thank you for listening and he wished all congregations would listen with such attention.

I must say I liked the little fellow. He was so eager, and unquenchable in his enthusiasm.

I asked him his business with Judder, the English Ambassador. And he withdrew from me slightly and his eyes took on a faraway look, and he said he must think before telling me, for in truth he did not trust me yet. I could see that he wanted to, but it was early days. He told me that he would see me again in two days. And when I asked where we would meet, he simply said that he would find me. Curious little fellow, he likes to weave an air of mystery about himself, when in fact his thought and intention are as plain as the brow on his face.

So I went about my wanderings. And I came to that Schiavoni place to look at those pictures done by Carpaccio, a painter who is much liked by the locals, for he did much about their daily lives, as well as their favourite saints such as Ursula.

I can see his skills, but he is not to my taste. He is too fantastic, as if he were always painting while half asleep, and the childhood demons that so tormented me were also guiding him, albeit into visions which are very different from mine, much sweeter and less strange. But as I say, I can see why he is admired.

He is very good on armour, and that is a subject that I too like, for it brings back those days in Milan at Uncle Dap's. I will work hard at that. I like the myriad reflections and blasts of light which fly off at different angles from the metal. And I like decorative engravings, they will be a great challenge to any man wishing to catch a real thing in paint.

He has one portrait of a youth all in black. His face is round and good-natured, and his sword looks like a broad length of cardboard. But the glory is the black armour. That must be especially difficult, I can see that, for the reflection of light off shiny black metal is altogether different from other colours. I want to get back to my colours to try out some of his effects on some scraps of canvas. I will have a man in black armour later in one of my own pictures. Perhaps a straight portrait, perhaps a soldier at the foot of the crucifixion, we shall see.

Then in one of the paintings I was detained by a wonderful little dog, all lively as if his whole body was wriggling, and with a wet black nose. I do not know what kind of dog they call it, it is the sort of tiny creature that is popular with old ladies to put in their laps, to keep them warm in winter.

I looked at it so long, I almost believed that it was alive, and I could step into the painting and pat its head and throw a lump of food for it, and get it to bark. I will get a dog, I am resolved. Not I think one of these silly little ones, for well-rendered though he is, he is not a dog for my taste. I will get a big black dog, who will respond to my call, and my call alone. I will teach him tricks and he will keep me company in a world where none else will. I like dogs better than people. Cats, too, although I am less sure about them.

His paintings of St Ursula are completely dotty, but then so is the story as far as I can make it out. She went off with eleven thousand virgins on some mad quest, and they all got killed by Huns, that'll teach them. And then she refused to yield her virginity to some Hun leader so he shot her with a bow and arrow. The eleven thousand virgins are not quite to my taste, but I could do something with a girl who has an arrow in her. Perhaps I will return to it some day.

I left and while I was walking alongside a canal, not far from Montin's, musing on the dog and the virgins, something strange happened. Some music had crept past me from across the water, unannounced, and taken me by surprise. I had stopped at a corner, to get my bearings, and the night was drawing on, which incidentally is my favourite time, and there was little light save for a flicker from a distant torch as someone wended their way home. And, as I stopped and looked about me, I suddenly realized that I had been listening to the music the past minute or so, without taking it in. Normally, I would walk on, and take it for granted. But there was something about it that anchored me where I stood and took my senses over. I was bewitched.

It was a violin that someone was playing in an upstairs room, and I could not move one foot in front of the other while they carried on playing. And after some little while, I realized that I did not even know what they were playing, but my cheeks were wet with tears, and I found myself leaning slightly against the wall, and trying to breathe easier. I was not crying exactly, it just felt as though my eyes were leaking. And then the player made a false note, and so went back a few bars and took it up again. And normally a break like that would split my mood, but it did not. I must have stood there a full fifteen minutes listening to that heavenly sound, before I had to leave for I could take no more.

The strange thing is that I am quite unmusical. I was not taught to read music, nor to play any kind of instrument, and up till now I have never even bothered to listen to one piece from one end to the other, but just take it all as background noise to some other activity. I do not hate it, but do not much think about it at all, in truth.

But now I am on to something I think. It would be nice to attach oneself to a musical group, say one in a palazzo or a church, for there are dozens of them around, and be able to go along and listen from time to time. All of that must be for the future, but never, ever will I forget that moment by the canal. It was as if a curtain were parted, and I was offered a glimpse of . . . what? Another world? Not exactly, for this one is strange enough for me. Some other way of being, or thinking, perhaps. It was a little split or tear in time, when the heavens open, and you are not quite who you thought you were. Nor ever will be again, though it is hard to hold on to those moments.

And try as hard as you like, you can never will it into being. As I discovered later, you must make yourself open to such things, and just pray that they will come to you. And if you stay open, then they will come, they will, believe me. For I have seen such visions as would strike you blind.

It occurred to me as I walked home that I should have knocked on the door and inquired as to who was playing and what the music was. But I knew I could not have done so then, and nor could I retrace my steps either, for the spell was broken. Yet I determined to go back at some time in my stay, for that fiddle player had stolen my heart and I wanted it back.

I never did return to that musician. Perhaps I will one day. Or perhaps I shall leave it as a mystery, I do not know. But

I do know that fifteen years later, I could still hum that tune, even though that was the first and only time I had heard it. I have hummed it to other musicians but none can tell me what the piece is, nor who wrote it. Perhaps it is better I do not know. I only inquire from time to time about it, and am not pursuing the knowledge very hard. But in my quieter moments, and especially if I am troubled, I like to hum it to myself. It soothes me.

Bruno found me, all right, as he said he would. He must have been following me around. But then this place is so small that if you lived here you would always be running into people you knew. I am not sure that I like that entirely. I don't want everyone knowing my business. Secrets are necessary to the best of lives. Only the very dull do not have secrets. And I have some very big ones indeed up my sleeve.

He waved his arms and beamed and took me into an *osteria* for its *ombra*, for it was the middle of a sunny morning, and we needed some shade, and we shared a little of the local red wine, which is very fine. They must ship it in from the mainland, for there were no vines in Venice that I could see. Bruno said that there were some, out on an outlying island, very swampy and malaria-ridden, with snakes too, lots of them. I took his word for it, but then Bruno tells me he flies with angels and converses with finny things from the vasty deep, and I take his word on that too, or rather I do not dispute it with him.

I can see that he does not think for one minute that he is convincing me. And I can see that he really doesn't mind. He just loves to talk, and I must admit I like to listen to him, he is so entertaining. Even the stuff about angels I can let slide by me. From someone else, I would tell him to shut his stupid mouth and box his ears he was so boring, but not fantastical little Bruno.

He first said that he was very sorry, and begged my pardon for not trusting me the other day. I said that it was nothing at all, and please think no more on it, for I would not trust me either. No, no, said Bruno, I am sure you are a trustworthy fellow, for you are close-mouthed and do not speak just for the sake of hearing your voice. No, it was just that he was worried about betraying confidences.

'For I am working a little for the French,' he said, sotto voce, leaning over his *bicchiere* of wine and breathing in my face. He had sweetened his breath with a bay leaf.

'Good for you,' I said, 'I care for them a lot more than I care for the Spanish.' It seemed all right to speak quite openly, here in the good Republic of Venice, about such matters, but Bruno looked about and raised his finger to his mouth in warning.

'For the French at present are Huguenot, which is a Protestant religion,' said Bruno.

'I know that,' I said, 'I am not a dolt.' And again he was

off, all apologies and saving my face. And I raised my hand and said, 'Get to the point.'

And he duly obliged. The gist of it all was that he had travelled all over Europe, lecturing on his magick and astrology and astronomy and alchemy and God knows what else besides, but mainly on the teachings of the ancient Egyptian sage Hermes Trismegistus, whose writings contained all the knowledge that was necessary for mortal man to know. I have heard of the man, though I know nothing of his teachings. But I do know that it is best not to know too much about him, for he was born before Christ and cannot therefore be a truly righteous man, at least according to our priests.

Anyway Bruno had given talks in Prague and to the Prussians and to the French King Henri of Navarre, and it was with Henri that he had found the most agreement and interest. And Bruno had been sold on the whole idea of Protestantism. For they were a tolerant religion and did not burn people like him at the stake, which the Vatican certainly would if they ever found out about what he was preaching.

I mean, you know and I know that all that is nonsense of the first water, but just let a Jesuit hear it and his nasty hook nose goes all twitchy and he starts shrieking 'heresy' at the top of his celibate voice, and before you know it they are tearing strips of flesh off your bum with red-hot irons, without any legal warrant, and burning you in the name of God.

Not Bruno, not my little Bruno, they won't get him while I'm around. I tousled his hair, and bought another drink of the red, and he carries on, bashing away about turning base metals to gold, and how the stars' courses in the heavens did mirror our paths here below, and how man is truly God-like, for everything above has its mirror image here below on earth. And how the earth is not the centre of the universe, but travels around the sun with other planets.

Whoa, I tell you flat out, I didn't like the sound of that last bit. That is exactly what they will start using the bastinado for, just especially for *you*. But he was babbling on, so I let him.

I do not think he is very involved with politics, but it seems that he is carrying messages for the French to and fro, wherever he goes, and he certainly goes all over the place. His current scheme is the importation from England of Protestant Bibles and prayer books into Venice, which he is effecting with the help of French money and the English Ambassador Judder, who piles them all up in a storeroom at his ambassadorial palazzo, and hands them out to whoever will take them.

I do not think Judder will get into much trouble, nor Bruno. But by the same token, I do not think he will convert many either. The Venetians are Catholics, but only in the sense that everyone around here is. They are not very sharp about their religion and, indeed, have such a world-weariness about them that you could probably conduct an cannibalistic black mass under their noses and not raise much excitement. *Nil admirare* is their watchword. Still, let him try if it keeps him happy. I always did like a man with an enthusiasm.

Plus, he likes me to fuck him when we get home of an evening. Well, there's a surprise. I did tell you he had been defrocked, didn't I?

Later he asked me if I would carry packets and letters for him, for he often needed things delivered that he did not want to be caught carrying. I suppose if I had been a different sort of man, I would have given that one some thought, but I do not much care what anyone thinks of me, so I said yes, whatever he liked, for indeed I was genuinely fond of him, and would do such things out of kindness for a friend, whatever the political meaning. Besides a painter is always carrying stuff around in a wallet, scraps of paper and bits of charcoal, maybe a small travelling palette and even small panels of wood. So a letter here or there wouldn't make any difference.

Political men, though, are a different matter. I hate them all. You can float them all out to sea in a leaky vessel and watch it sink and go down with all hands, and the world will carry on just as it had before and not be one jot worse off.

I continued in Venice awhile, even though I had exhausted the place of all the things I wanted to see. One thing I never tired of, though, and that was the coming of evening. It is my favourite time, as I think I have told you, but here in Venice it is fabulous.

I have always preferred the dusk. Night is not just a different time, it is a different place. And the change from light to dark is one of the few things that can calm me. Here in Venice, the evening sun turns coral and the long light shakes across the milk-green waters in a meeting of colours that turns my mind from its usual fret and calms me.

And I often stand outside my quarters, in a narrow *calle*, and watch until it is all dark, for there are no torches on the wall here, and no travellers pass by. But it is never fully black. The reflections of the water play in endless waves across the walls, like phosphorous serpents, and when there is no moon, even the stars can pick out the cracks between the stones of Venice. I have known nights black as pitch, but can always make things out, for my night vision is good, and I am not afraid of the dark. Darkness gives me light.

That is what I took from Venice: the dark, some black armour, and a dog. Oh, and a liking for Bruno. I will help him as he asks and will see him again soon.

I lie. Of course I took other stuff too, such as colour technique; and being true to what you have in front of you, rather than tricking it up with fake holiness or costume frippery; and not drawing the subject first, in the way the Florentines do, but painting straight to canvas. But that is all trade secrets, we don't talk about that. Armour, dark and dog is all you'll get from me if we talk, and let it stand you in good stead.

Rome

Rome is the only place to be if you are a painter. At other times it was Florence, and at yet other times Venice and yet other times . . . I do not know, hopeless provincial shit-holes like Perugia or Urbino I expect, places you have heard of but never want to visit. Right now, as the end of this hundred-year approaches, Rome is the one place to be.

Upon my way to Rome, I wandered over my native Lombardy and saw many paintings, none of which I admired much, bar one by Campi, which was a wondrous thing of night and fire. I can't remember the title. Indeed I never knew it. Words do not interest me. But a good picture I never forget. It is as if the painter had thrust his brushes through my eye sockets and daubed his image permanently on the back of my eyeballs, there to remain for ever imprinted. I can conjure up any memory I wish simply by associating the thought with a particular scene or person in a painting. I believe learned men do the same sort of thing when they wish to memorize a book by associating the thought in it with certain rooms in their house.

And my visual memory is unfailing. I may not remember the names of even my most recent of friends too well, but place me in a landscape that I have not seen nor been near for twenty years and I will tell you the next bend in the road and what lies beyond. And I can quote whole sentences from a book, not by recalling the words themselves, but by remembering where the sentence was on the page, and what its shape was. It is a strange gift, and most men do not understand it. And it can be a curse, cluttering up your mind with all sorts of nonsense that has no business being there. To be able to forget things would be a great relief to me, and more valuable than remembering things. Perhaps age will bring me this relief. Strong drink is the only remedy at the moment. My brain is often so crammed with pictures that I can only sleep when drunk.

That Campi was good, though. I can use that shade effect, and maybe the composition and placing of his models too. Men will borrow from me one day, I am sure of it. So, meantime, I will take what I want from my forebears and make use of it.

I had a living to make, and a reputation too, and so I went to the only place a painter could go.

I entered Rome from the north, through serious bandit country and starving farms, and immediately I knew I had found my home. The streets, the new buildings, the very stones seemed to welcome me, and the skies were warm and bright. It had been sacked not so long ago, by the Spanish and the French, who were too cowardly to do it themselves but had employed German mercenaries to do their dirty work. That would have been in the time of my grandfather. But now it was rebuilt to a glorious state, and everywhere there were new buildings, shining among the ruins like a new piece of gold on a hill of shit.

Succeeding Popes had outdone themselves in recreating a centre for artistic excellence, and had not stinted in hiring the best at whatever prices they asked for. They had even taken on Michelangelo. (My namesake, not me. Not yet.) What with the new religion in the north breathing hellfire down their neck, they had to do all they could to keep the faithful rounded up and contented. And fearful too. The Inquisition was growing ever stronger, and popping up everywhere unannounced. No one ever got warning or expected a call from them. And there was something new called the Order of Jesuits, which I didn't like the sound of. Listening to tavern talk gave you the distinct impression that the modern Church was favouring the stick over the carrot.

Well, they can shove that up their arse, and suck on this.

I looked up an old uncle who was something in the Church and he found me cheap lodgings with a mean little man, Pucci, who fed me nothing but salad in the evenings. I endured him for a few months before finding somewhere else, though I took the small pleasure on the last day of grabbing him by the hair and stuffing a radicchio into his mouth, so he was gagged. Then I pinched his nose, so he could not draw breath, till his eyes popped out on their stalks and he fainted. The taffeta punk.

I called it a day then, feeling better humoured than I usually do, because I had somewhere to go to.

After I left Pucci's I earned small money in sweat shops which were churning out bits of art. They were nothing more than cheap little gewgaws to adorn a maid's bedroom wall or a washerwoman's pantry, an ancient Greek boy's face or a man in a soldier's helmet – I could do as many as three in one day. You might think that I would despise such work, and indeed I did so in general for it was no more than hack stuff. But part of me did not. After all, it did not pretend to be other than what it was. It assumed no airs or graces. And no time is ever wasted for an artist when he is painting, no matter how quick or easy the finished thing. For he is ever moving forward in his work. And today's discoveries soon become yesterday's cheap trick and tomorrow brings on a new way of doing things.

I give you an example. It took me much time to be able to capture a reflection of a patch of light on a wall or on some object as seen through a glass pitcher of water. The problem for me was mainly one of distortion but also of rendering pure sunlight using only colour. The secret is in the background contrast, but this I discovered simply by returning again and again to the problem in my little hack works.

She probably doesn't know it, but somewhere there is a Roman fishwife with a sentimental little view of some flowers on a table tacked to her bedroom wall, which contains what future scholars will call 'a major breakthrough in the technique of the great Caravaggio'. Or she might throw it away next year when she tires of it, and it will be eaten by the pigs in their swill. Hah.

Better that than adorn a smooth diplomat's salon as proof only of his wealth and standing and then be carried off as plunder when the neighbouring country sacks his palace.

Then I joined Cesari's workshop. He was something of a swell at that time, with pointy little mustachios, and well connected. Clement, the Pope, was using him to decorate miles and miles of pious walls, paying him I expect by the yard. He wanted me to join in his team of painters, who were sweating away on these grand projects like so many scaffolders on a building site. But I would not. I was loath to tell him that I did not do frescoes, because I did not want him to think me deficient in training. I could do them all right, it's just that I did not want to. I am not entirely sure why. Let me think.

I do not like daubing onto wet plaster. It makes me shudder. Something to do with the texture sets my teeth grinding, in the way some men cannot abide a cat's fur or a rat. Then there is the milkiness of the colours when they dry. Effeminate stuff for whey-faced prelates. And then . . . I know what it is now.

It is the fact that it is there, fixed for all time on the wall, and unable to be moved. Why should I dislike that so? I do not know, but I do. I want my art transportable, and, above all, destructible. You don't like my picture? Then smash it against the wall, and tear the canvas to ribbons with your knife. Erase it utterly till it offends your eye no more. You paid me well enough for it, it is yours to do with as you please. But will you? Will you? I don't think so.

After all, it might have future value. It might please your descendants, or better still the big dealers who will pay your descendants, or you might settle your gambling debts with it, or you might use it as collateral for a big business deal, or you might steal it and ransom it back to its owner or their insurance agents or . . . any number of possible things. But not if it's sunk in plaster on some monastery wall, where only an earthquake will dislodge it. Paintings on canvas are just like big banknotes. I like that idea.

So I didn't do much for Cesari except quick easel stuff. There were bowls of fruit and flowers in vases on tables and so on. Stuff that nobody had ever bothered to paint until recently and so had not even thought to give the subject a name. I should not think they will ever bother again either. It is boring. I needed to paint people. But could not afford a model.

Cesari used to take his painters from the workshop off to the ruins, and hold forth about the classical statuary. He even insisted that I go with the group one day, and so I went, rather than fall out with him. Dear God, but it was tedious stuff, all those bare white limbs in graceful poses. Can ancient Greece really have looked like that? It must have been insufferable. While Cesari held forth about proportion and the golden mean and suchlike, I studied a group of ugly sightseers, shuffling about the Circo Massimo, where they used to hold chariot races, listening to their guide and taking in the culture. They were a spotty lot, all hunched and sweaty and bent-faced. And they were all I needed, and I said half-aloud, 'They are all that I need.' I almost sketched them there and then, just to make a point to Cesari, but did not, for I will not break a rule of a lifetime just to make cheap points. Cesari spotted me studying them anyway, and sighed heavily and left me there. I approached one of them, a bald, old, wrinkly man, who yet retained some good-looking qualities and a face that showed much strength. I told him to come to Cesari's studio sometime and leave me an address where I might reach him. He is my idea of a saint. Not that I have painted a saint yet. But I will, I will, warts and all.

My how my mind does run on. I never thought of myself as a thinker. It is amazing how illness compacts the mind. Or perhaps it is those herbs my doctor keeps forcing between my lips.

So I painted myself. I do not know why I had not thought of it previously. I was miserable for so long because I could not afford a model, when I had one standing right beside me. All I needed was a glass.

The grapes were beginning to wrinkle and decay, giving off that smell of rotten sweetness that can repel and attract at the same moment. I too had been rotting inside. A bout of malaria, which was to dog me for the rest of my life, gotten in the swamp outside Rome, had left my skin yellow, and thus I painted it. As to the look on my face, which made men recoil before they could stop themselves, well . . . I can do nothing about that. As in life, so in my art.

Because of the grapes they called it a Bacchus. It was no such thing, but I played up to it anyway by adding a crown of vine leaves about my head. Having dissembled so, by passing it off as a classical study, I got some money for it. Not much, but enough to tell me I was on my way. If I was going to get anywhere, I knew I had best adjust to the notion that I was going to have to paint classical or religious subjects. Greek boys and saints, that is what the state and the Church, pederasts and celibates all of them, wanted, and it was the state and the Church that paid good money and gave a man a name. *But I would paint them my way, not theirs.*

I had a small spell in the hospital, for some ailment or other I have forgotten, perhaps it was when the horse kicked me. I have never been too mindful of my health. But what I do remember was that neither Cesari nor his brother came to see me, not even when I was better. That seems to me an unkindness I had not deserved, especially since I had worked so hard for them. So I did not go back to Cesari's studio.

I have no truck with those touchy souls who demand respect for simply being alive. Most people have no right to any respect at all. But if a man does something which earns my admiration and respect, then no matter who he is, I will not stint.

You may hate me on sight, I do not care at all. But if I have done you some kindness worthy of your respect, then your respect for that action is all I ask. Hate me all you want, but treat me as I have treated with you, accordingly.

The Cesaris did not. They were disloyal. They were not the last people to behave like that in my life either, but they got off lightly. I have killed for less.

I did a few other young boys, in poses, either myself or, more often, my good friend Minitti. He has the face of an angel, and a nature to boot. God knows what he is doing with me. It can only be pity, though I do not like to ask, not wishing to upset matters. The thing is, I adore him, but he'll have none of me.

Normally, if I couldn't have him I would forget him, go get drunk, and have someone else. But Minitti . . . I don't know, he was but a boy of sixteen, so sweet, so very innocent, I felt he needed protecting and so I was like his older brother.

But my ways were too wild for him, and he had no taste for gambling and whoring such as I need. Still, I will not abandon him. He reminds me of a spaniel dog.

I always liked dogs more than men.

Then I found a gypsy girl who had the right look about her. Attractive, erotic too, but mischievous. And I painted her reading young Minitti's palm. Except that he is so taken by her charming looks, poor silly boy, that he doesn't see her slipping the ring from his finger. Neither does the viewer for a little while, unless he be especially sharp. I was pleased with the figures, though it was a simple painting, and I am not always pleased with my efforts, but this was worthy of me. And I stuck with the cheats I found at my usual tavern as a topic and my next painting was of two cardsharps cheating a boy. I gave the kibbitzer a glove with a hole at the fingertip, a touch I was most pleased with for it looked most real. It was taken from my own glove, which has ten holes all in a row.

No matter, for the picture was my making.

Del Monte

How is the world ruled and how do wars start?
Diplomats tell lies to journalists and then believe what they read.

Karl Kraus. *Aphorisms and more aphorisms (1909)*

It was hawked in the street, outside the Palazzo Madama, the place where Cardinal del Monte lives; and the Cardinal saw it, liked it, found me and took me in. At last, my due. I could buy new gloves now, all that I wanted, but I didn't bother. It was the credit I craved. I shall never forget that moment when his steward approached me with the news and brought me to the door of the palazzo. I gave a little jump in the air.

Del Monte was an easy man. The sort that most men like immediately. He was a diplomat, born from a family of diplomats, but he had none of that unctuousness that so many diplomats exude, that desire to be liked at all costs. Del Monte seemed so well fixed in his own character that he could tolerate all manner of things in other men. God knows my own behaviour, my drinking, my bad language, my shouting and brawling would have driven anyone else to expel me from the house, but del Monte just smiled and smiled, and that was enough to chastise me and mend my ways temporarily. He really had the sweetest nature and not once did I ever see him unjustly angry.

And I gave him something in return, I think. What did he see in me? I think he saw the bad boy that he had never been. The bad boy inside that was forever pushing against his better nature and urging to be let loose. When young, he was a favourite of the head man of the de' Medici rulers in Florence, and, even from just when his voice broke, the older man had always confided everything in the young del Monte. What a privilege, and what a burden! Forever the courtier, forever on guard. I think del Monte saw in me that bit of himself he had never been allowed to let rip when young. I was what every man would be. If only they dared. Perhaps this is the basis of friendships, I do not know. Each man seeks in another that part of himself which is missing. Thus do people make themselves more whole.

I wish I could make myself whole with Minitti, he is so pretty. But he still will have none of me. Though he likes me well enough. The Cardinal even took him in too and let him live with us in the Madama. God love the man, he was a prince. It was only his early alliance with the French that many years later cost him the papacy. Rome, the Vatican, the Holy Church, all of Christendom itself would have been a better, kinder place had he been given his chance. And what art we would have made for the world. For del Monte was not just a patron, he knew what was what in paintings. I could talk to him of colour pigments and brushwork and perspective and so on, and he in no way made a fool of himself. That is rare. Too often I have seen painters have to humble themselves before some rich prick. It is humiliating. Not with del Monte, though.

I knew his sexual tastes, but need not go into them here. Suffice to say that one of his favourite paintings was of a lute player swooning to the music, which is quite clearly printed in the foreground 'I love, I adore you'. Actually the painting had been ordered by Giustiniani, the banker who lived over the road, an odd choice for such a hard-driving man who loved nothing but hunting animals and finance. He came to bankroll the papacy itself but that is by the by. Del Monte loved the painting so much he was loath to let it go, and begged me do a copy. That is something I normally refuse, but I relented. Besides, Minitti looked so lovely, his eyes misted with tears of joy at the music. And I used one of the Cardinal's own lutes as a model for the cherub's instrument. He was keen on music.

He was keen on a lot of other things too. The young Galileo, along with his brother, was often to be found at the house. And I saw him give del Monte a brand-new brass telescope, all shiny, which was a mighty dangerous thing to do, what with the Inquisition having informers in every major household. To look up to the heavens was to tread dangerously close to God's work. And only the Inquisition are allowed to go about doing God's work for Him. You have to be very, very holy before you are allowed to torture and kill people within the law.

Those first few years at the Palazzo Madama were a strange time for me. I almost dwindled into domesticity. It was the first time, and it would be the last, when I knew some stability of the sort a well-set-up marriage can bring. We all quietly walked forward at a stately pace. Neither counting the days nor fretting about time lost, but steadily working and taking our ease and eating and drinking at regular hours. I must have been happy, for I never noticed, nor even thought of happiness. And I did some good stuff I reckon.

What broke things up a bit was a ceiling painting. I told everyone and made it known that I would never work in fresco, nor do anything but paint oil on canvas. I think I told you why.

But del Monte had bought a little summer house at Port Pinciani. He regretted the purchase quite soon afterwards because he wasn't terribly fond of the *casina* for some reason which I never fathomed. It always seemed a nice enough place to me, but then I run to no great taste in such matters. I bed down wherever I am, and all I need is a roof over my head and a place to shit and I am happy.

Still, del Monte bought this little folly mainly I think to conduct his alchemical experiments there, or maybe something a bit sexier, for he liked to stage little plays or masques, in which the female parts were played by pretty young boys. Nothing unusual in that, of course, but I must say that del Monte took a great deal of care in casting and rehearsing those pretty boys. Good luck to him.

He was very keen that I paint a mural on the ceiling. God rot him, he put it so nicely I let my guard slip and instead of scowling and turning on my heel, which I would normally do, I went ahead. Also, and this I did not tell him, there had been some nasty rumours among the town's painters that I could not do perspective. I have since learnt to ignore such gossip, but I was young then and easily stung. I knew I was the best, but had yet to establish my claim, and so I thought I had something to prove. Sink me, but young men are stupid. No man under thirty ought to be allowed to voice an opinion by law.

Anyway I took it on, and began preparing. The scaffolding was put up, and I got some assistants, Minitti included, to start grinding pigment and the plasterer came in, did his stuff all over the ceiling and told me he'd mixed it right so it would stay wet awhile, and then I got cracking, launched straight in, sloshing away left and right at about a good fast canter, faster than my normal pace anyway because I didn't want the bore of having to wet the plaster all over again if it dried. And it was coming on a treat. Three whacking great gods, Jove, Neptune, Pluto, all standing around looking like they owned the place and a nasty looking hound,

Cerberus, all teeth and whites around the eyes, which looked like it would have ripped your head off if you looked it in the eye too long.

And then the plaster began to dry and I hadn't finished, and before my eyes all the colours went off and looked milky. Fortunately I was standing at the base of the scaffolding, for I felt the blood begin to rise to my head again. I lifted up the whole tower and pushed it over so it collapsed and then picked up a couple of poles and jabbed at the ceiling so that the plaster was dislodged and then smeared cloths all over the paint. And then threw the stupid pigments all over the walls.

When I came to a few hours later they told me I had nearly killed one of my assistants with a piece of wood from the scaffolding tower. He was still unconscious from the blows to his head. I went to look at him, still very unsteady on my feet, and he was alive thank God, but black and blue. I have never felt remorse, indeed I do not know what men mean by it. But del Monte was less than pleased and chided me for it, and I knew for my own good that it was better that I never used assistants again. Nor try to do anything but intimate work on canvas with my brush and my oils. And not worry what men might say about my technique.

I can do perspective, of course. I have seen it all over the place and it's easy as pie. I had seen the Alberti brothers' stuff on the Vatican ceiling, where it all slips up the walls and onto the ceiling, and I could see immediately how to do it. There is even a mechanical way to cheat it if you want, with compasses and rulers and bits of string, but that is all for students, and I have no need of it. My eye is good and I can keep hold of the larger picture in my mind's eye while doing the miniature stuff.

So I went back to the ceiling and this time waited till the plaster dried and just threw on my oils and in no time at all there was as good a painting as I had ever done and much better than those wretched frescoes, all nice and gleaming new, the way that only oils can. So damn fresco to hell and back, because of the things it made me do. Never again would I touch the feeble stuff.

Neptune looks a touch like me, but with a bushier beard. And in the middle of them all I painted a celestial sphere, with a zodiac band across it, with some astrological rubbish about the sun being in Cancer, which del Monte showed me how to place, because he was born in Cancer, and it is his birth sign. Got to keep the old fool happy, I suppose.

What a thing. It's still there on the ceiling if you want to go and see it. I never did another one. Nor a subject like it neither. Three big male nudes all looking very businesslike with their tridents and vicious dog and a big seahorse. They all look quite ferocious, and have that air about them that looks as though they are spoiling for a fight.

Well, if they had been alive and had hung around with me for a year or so, they would have got their wish. And, as I will tell you soon, the murderous brawl I got into was so fearful, I could have done with a few gods on my side. Not to mention a dog.

The Cenci

'. . . horror and ugliness and filthiness of sin.'

Ruskin. Victorian art critic.

They killed the Cenci family, and I saw it. God, what a vile procession that made in the midday heat. The Pope even set up a special platform so he could perform a pre-execution mass in full view. Several people died in the press of the crowds, some said from the heat, some say it was a piece of scaffolding collapsed. Myself I think it was from disgust, not at the butchery, but the Pope's hypocrisy. Or else sexual excitement, for there was a lot of that about in the crowd. And up on the scaffold too.

First came Lucrezia, old Cenci's second wife and step-mother to the three children, also all accused. They said that they had bashed in Francesco Cenci's head with a hammer, then tossed him off a balcony. From what I knew of him, I can't say I blamed them. Lucrezia was weak from the tortures they had found it necessary to give her in order to extract a confession. They had tied her hands behind her, then suspended her by her wrists and dropped her from a height until she was brought up short by the rope. Both shoulders were dislocated. After some nine hours of this treatment she confessed to having murdered her husband. Well, you would too, wouldn't you? Likewise did the two sons, Giacomo, and Bernadino, who was only fifteen.

Only Beatrice, a beautiful and well-grounded girl of twenty, resisted confessing, although they claimed that she finally broke. I think this another lie from the Inquisition. No one else was present at her ordeal.

Lucrezia kept fainting, from a combination of her torture and the heat. Finally the executioner pulled her slack body up the scaffold, grabbed her hair and placed her unconscious head on the block. I noted that the blood flowed from her severed neck in a continuous stream, rather like thin ropes dangling from her head. I used that later in a *Judith and Holofernes* and a couple of other beheadings.

Lucrezia was followed by Beatrice, and the crowd was truly amazed by her behaviour. She comported herself like the holiest of men. She nothing common did, nor mean. Yet retained her air of defiance to the end. She laid her own head down upon the block as comely as a maid laying on a pillow to sleep. And when the axeman did his office, the crowd gave out only a low moan of pity and admiration.

I saw Vialardi, the spy, taking notes near the scaffold. No doubt some ambassador or prince will have hired this jackal to apprise them of the scene.

I do not know why Giacomo, the elder son, was treated

lower than a brute beast. No doubt that Jesuit who heads up the Inquisition had it in for him. I know that hook-nosed bastard. His name is Bellarmino, and if ever a man is headed straight for Dante's ninth circle of Hell it is he. He has no feelings, only an extra brain where his heart should be, stuffed full of pious hatred. Bellarmino doesn't just hand out the sentence, he likes to be present when it's carried out. Not that he ever gives away any pleasure he might have at watching the impenitent suffer. He just sits there stony-faced throughout, without a twitch disturbing his big-nosed features. I think I prefer those sadists who get a hard-on from watching people suffer, and always gather to gloat at these events. They at least are honest about their tastes.

Throughout the procession they tortured Giacomo with hot irons, scorching and tearing at his flesh. The smell of burned meat wafted over the crowd. Then one of the executioners whom I had been sketching, a brute of a man with twisted features and a look of exalted lust, clubbed down his victim within sight of the scaffold and cut his throat. The blood poured from his severed neck, yet he was still alive while the gang of butchers set about dismembering him. His limbs and the quartered body were put on display to the crowd. And later put on spikes until near midnight. I noted the look on the face of the executioner. It was one of ferocious lust. I will use it for a 'Flagellation'. Or maybe a 'Crucifixion', if I ever get around to painting one.

Bernadino, being only fifteen, and therefore deemed too

young to die, had been sentenced to a life in the galleys. I tell you, it would have been better for him that he was burned alive there and then. Those galleys are no joke. He was made to watch his family being put to death, and every time he fainted was revived with some relish by a priest from the Inquisition, the better to enjoy the festival.

All the while, the Pope was watching the spectacle and openly weeping. I have often seen him weep. Indeed, I looked into his eyes once, and I tell you: watch his hands more closely and only there you will see what is in his mind. His eyes lie.

And you wonder why I hate priests?

I hate priests with the same intensity that most people hate lawyers. But I do not hate lawyers, for I once met a most valiant one. I did a portrait of him some time after the execution of the Cenci. He was a brave man and quite without vanity for he had lost an eye in a fight and his left face-side was somewhat disfigured. Yet he bid me paint him full face, wounds and all. As I was painting, he told me that he had tried to represent the young Beatrice to the Pope. While the stepmother had indeed had her husband killed, nonetheless, if ever man deserved to die it was he. He had roundly abused them all, and not just with violence, although plenty enough of that, but had committed incest on both his daughter and his sons.

And they say I have a tortured brain!

Not only that, but he had had to pay off at least half of his fabled wealth in order to have a charge of sodomy suppressed. Nearly 250,000 *scudi*, straight to the Pope's coffers.

The lawyer, who was called Prospero, had gone to the Pope with the story of the wretched Beatrice's rape by her father, and had been shouted out of the Holy Father's chambers and threatened with prosecution for daring to represent so wicked a woman. So much for justice.

Once the Cenci were safely dead and the various pieces of their bodies interred, their estates were forfeit to the Papacy and their biggest piece of land, their villa at Terranova, was sold for nearly nothing to an Aldobrandini. He is one of the Pope's nephews. The money made went into the Vatican coffers.

Such was the public outrage that laws were passed forbidding anyone to mention the Cenci family or defame the prosecuting of them or 'use vile tongues in public places'. All of this I got from my lawyer friend, who is most brave and has no reason to lie.

And you still wonder why I hate priests?

Fillide

When you want to see if your painting corresponds overall to the thing painted from life, get a mirror and reflect the living thing in it, and compare the reflection with your painting . . . (and if you've done it right) your painting too will look like a natural thing seen in a mirror.

Leonardo. *The Book of Painting*

I met her in an *albergo*, and I knew I was in trouble. I had seen her around earlier, as a matter of fact, but had not really registered her in my mind. It is often like that with obsession. One minute they are nothing but a common tart you wouldn't cross the road for even it she was giving it away free. The next moment they are a goddess who walks the earth on silver sandals. Or so young men tell me. It's not like that with me, of course. Oh, she cast a spell all right, but with stuff like that I can always keep my head. The rages? I don't know exactly, but it's not a woman that brings them on.

No, it took a few meetings, but suddenly there it was before me; exactly the face that I wanted. Or rather, the look. Before it had been men, but now it was this woman. How best can I describe her?

Fillide was a problem.

She was one of the Malandroni family, a modest lot from Siena, but she moved to Rome upon her father's death and put herself to work, doing what any woman does. She made herself rich in the trade, and eventually she acquired the patronage of the nobleman Giulio Strozzi, who wished to marry her. You may find that surprising, but she had become high-flown in her ways. She reminded men of the old days, when the great 'honest courtesans' had been the pride of Rome. They were cultivated and witty and lived in the most sumptuous palaces. Fillide had something about her, a quality not easily caught or explained. And I was not surprised about Strozzi's plans either. For I loved Fillide too. As far as I ever loved a woman.

She was dark, with extravagant hair. Large eyes, a straight nose . . . I could go on but these are no more than features you could find on a thousand whores all within spitting distance of the Palazzo Madama. What arrested me was a wantonness which shone in her brow, a cleverness which suggested that she was shrewd enough to behave like a man. She took her pleasures when and where she wanted, and she was not one to give in to the fancies that she saw in other, silly girls. Oh, she had something about her all right. And I caught it. Just look on my portraits of her, you will see what I am getting at.

It was when Strozzi commissioned a portrait of her from me that I got to know her better. I did not idealize her, as the Venetians and Titian might have done, but painted her as she was. God's blood, but she was handsome. Even her name spoke of class, not like the usual street girls' names such as Maddalena or Angelica. I painted her in one of her luxurious dresses of scarlet and green taffeta, shot with gold, and with the jewels and clustered earrings that she loved so much. And I caught, just so, her brass-necked stare. She could make a monk renounce his vows with that look. Heavy-lidded, dark-eyed whore that she was, she turned it on me once and my hand shook and my mouth went dry and I knew I had to have her.

I used to keep a few gold coins in my purse. If one of the beggars I often used as models started to complain about keeping still for so long in an awkward pose, I would toss him a coin to shut him up. It was the end of a hot afternoon, I was concentrating on Fillide's ruched sleeve, and she turned her gaze on me, as full and wanton as a bitch in heat. Without thinking I threw her a gold coin. She caught it, bit into it, laughed and tossed the coin back at me. She could have earned ten times more for an hour spent on her back, she said.

'Then do so,' I said, 'though it will not make you famous.'

'I am already famous,' she said. And that was true.

'Then it will not make you immortal,' I said.

'None can make me immortal,' she said.

'I can,' I said. 'Just stand still.'

Then I moved quickly on her.

She laughed again and swirled her long skirt about her as she dismounted the dais, and began to walk away. By accident, I trod on the hem of her skirt. It tore and came half away, and she wore no underskirts. She paused, and said no word of dismay, not even an intake of breath, but undid her sash and tore the rest of the skirt away to reveal her bare legs and belly and a mass of dark moss. I gripped her shoulders and kissed her, and she locked her arms about my neck and lifted herself up, and in I thrust.

God's teeth, but she was tight. A full-grown woman, with the gulley of a young nun. I could see why men would pay her good money. And the grip she exerted over them, and Ranuccio and Strozzi too, by all in heaven, was surely this. Perhaps her trench was muscled like a young man's arm, I do not know. I do not like to look on women's parts. They are ugly and put me off what I would there intend, just as surely as if her face were ugly too.

As I have said, she took her pleasures like a man, when and where she pleased, but there was something about her that won . . . something in me, almost my heart. Although never, ever would I admit that to her. She could make a man waste his life, leave his chosen path and lose all just to be near her and smell her. She could ruin a man, and be pleased to do so. So I fucked her till she was spent and limp and mewing happily, the way they do, and left her without having come myself. If she wanted my sperm, she could take payment for it like any other whore. Till then, I will keep whole and entire unto myself. Not one word of what I felt would she ever hear. I'll have no bride but my paintings.

You think me strange? Inhuman, perhaps? You haven't heard the half of it.

When I pulled out of her, I grabbed her by the hair and made her lick me clean with her tongue. Her teeth nipped me, not accidentally I think, so I hit her. She cursed at me, and spat, so I hit her again, not on the face, but hard across the shoulder and sent her sprawling. And I pissed all over her. 'Be back here tomorrow, at the same time,' I said. And indeed she did return as I ordered. She wasn't mine yet, there was no surrender in her eyes, no craving. Not yet, anyway. Just give me time.

So I made her stand even longer at the next session, and she did not complain. She knew she could never win me by submitting. But what she did not know was that she would never win me by being my equal either. No woman could be that. I use them, and then I forget them and use another, and nothing else will do for me. Run after a woman? I'd as soon chase a greased pig.

The portrait was a success, and Strozzi paid me well for it. I spent much of it on whores, to calm the rage in me; the rest on gambling, to stoke it up. I like my rage. It separates me from the rest. The ones who do not dare.

Ranuccio

And to be boy eternal

Shakespeare. *A Winter's Tale. (1610)*

Ranuccio, then.

He was a member of the Tomassoni family, and men hated them. They were all soldiers. Not that that was unusual at that time in Rome. The wars with Spain were over and the place was thick with warriors. From Flanders and from Hungary, Croatia and Slovenia, they came limping back, scarred, diseased, lame, but full of fire. They had nothing to do of an evening but drink and play at cards or with a tennis ball. The disputes were many and were resolved by steel.

Many times I was arrested for carrying a sword, but I claimed dispensation because of my position in the service of the Cardinal del Monte, in whose house I lived. I even carried my sword at night which was more strictly illegal. And if the place was well lighted I would have a boy carry it for me. That act alone put me in prison several times, but it saved my life more than once in this city of drunken mercenaries.

And I always had my dagger about me. It is more precious to me than any other thing in the world. I even have it close when I sleep. Closer than the whore who might be beside me.

Ranuccio's father had been in the French wars, and was in Paris on the night of St Bartholomew, when they slew all the Huguenots. No doubt he took his part in the bloody deeds. He is a good Catholic, after all, and none can murder like a Catholic when the smell of a heretic makes his nose twitch. His two eldest sons were both commended for their bravery elsewhere. But bravery turns to thuggery when there is nothing to occupy a soldier. They walked the streets of Rome as if they owned them. They swaggered and slouched and took turns at devising new insults for those that stood in their way. And I loved them for it.

Ranuccio was new to the game but he had good masters in his family. His sneer was legendary. I heard him once from two streets away swear that he would 'burn the balls off this whoreson scum', and turned the corner to find him with his hand on the pommel of his undrawn sword, and two men fleeing past me, their faces pale with fright. Oh, he had *sprezzatura*, all right. He could call out the Devil himself and make him flinch. Such braggadocio. Such style.

They were, as I have said, a family of some standing and they went under the protection of the Farnese clan, which is only to say one of the most powerful families in Rome.

You had better think twice before showing your naked steel to them.

But I never, never think twice about anything. Men said I was impulsive beyond all good reason. You may even say that that was my downfall; but it is in my nature and you cannot change your nature. Nor would I ever wish to, let the dice fall where they may.

And I spit on the wary. Wariness is like a disfiguring disease. I even love Judas more than St Thomas. I have painted both of them but Judas is my favoured one. Wary, doubting Thomas I showed shoving his finger into Christ's wound like an impotent dotard fingering a whore's gulley. But Judas I gloried in. I used an old man as a model for Judas, a man with a face mottled from too much drink. I always got into trouble for that; for using common people as models. They, the priests and my patrons, told me it was profane. Hah. Of course it was profane. That's the point.

Judas at least knew his place in the scheme of things. He dared to do what no one else would do: call down ignominy and hatred upon his own head for all eternity. Ah, to be universally despised. To never know a friend and be spat on wherever he was found. A man could hold his head up.

I first had Ranuccio some little while after the turn of the new century. It was spring and the nights were becoming a shade lighter. But it was dark on that night. We knew each other well enough. I had often seen him strolling about

Piazza Navona, barging younger men out of the way, or bit-ing his thumb at one or other from a rival family.

We had been gaming in the Tavern of the Wolf. The *sbirri*, those useless scum, had been patrolling the inns, looking for some ill-begotten oaf that someone had informed on, so that they might beat him and take him to their cells, and make him inform on others. The authorities wish to clean up the streets, yet they are too mean to invest in a force of good men. Instead they hire creepers, back-stabbers, sly down-at-heelers and call them police. I have known baby-rapists more noble than most *sbirri*.

They burst in the door on us with swords drawn, but we beat them back with whatever weapon that came to hand. I found a length of wood, I think it was a broom handle, that I used as a cudgel. And Ranuccio picked up a three-legged stool and split the skull of one of the police spies and broke another's arm at the elbow. You could hear the crack of the joint clear across the room, and the man's screams. Others joined in and one man at least was badly wounded from a sword. But we beat them off and they retreated into the night, muttering curses though none too loudly, cowards that they were. The landlord had seen such things often enough and simply brought up more bottles for the crew, but Ranuccio and I found ourselves outside in the alley, panting for breath, our blood up and nothing to answer for it.

It was then I knew what he wanted. No look passed

between us, no sign was given, but I knew. I gripped his arm and turned him to the wall, pushed him forward and had him there. A lick of spit and I entered him hard, and he grunted loudly and panted and then spent very quick. He was still sweating from the fight and he smelt like a tomcat. I had my dagger out and pressed it to his shoulder, only lightly, but enough to draw blood, and I licked the blood as it flowed from his muscle. The smell is what I remember to this day. The smell of blood and of shit. Perhaps that is all that men are composed of.

When I had done, he hawked and spat against the wall, and turned to me as he buttoned up. There was satisfaction in his eyes, and something more curious, something I could not make out. I came to know that look later. I put it in my paintings, when he sometimes did pose for me, and in the face of other men too. It was triumph, as if it had been he that had taken me in such rough fashion. Others who might have seen us, bystanders to our act, might call what I did rape. But not he, nor I.

I call it victory.

How I came to kill him, I will tell you later.

Bruno on Fire

Shadow tempers light . . . Shadows don't dissolve but keep
and protect the light in us, and lead us toward knowledge and memory.

Giordano Bruno. *The Shadows of Ideas*

They burned Bruno, and I saw it.

The Cardinal del Monte did so much for me, I wish him
very well indeed. I have said that he had a sweet nature, but
it was more complex than that. I think he genuinely liked
to see others happy. He would take delight in fixing things,
and thanks to his diplomatic nature and his large circle of
friends and acquaintances and others, he could usually effect
almost any change in the affairs of men. A simple smile
here, a favour done there, and after only a few years he had
built an enormous structure of people who were only too
anxious to help him. It was strange because he actually
had comparatively little power. People could not rely on
advancement from him. True, he was a cardinal, but he was
not rich. Nor did he have the Pope's ear. And the loose talk
that he might himself succeed to the Papacy when old was

defeated by his alliance with the French authorities, in preference to the Spanish.

But still, as I say, people liked him and liked to please him, and he likewise.

The Contarelli chapel, just over the road from his palazzo, was becoming something of a scandal. The chapel was in the Church of San Luigi dei Francesi, or St Louis of the French, if you prefer, as Bruno always put it. It was the church built in order to let any visiting or resident Frenchies worship among their own kind. It had been paid for by one Mathieu Cointrel, a Frenchman, though he often went by the Italianate name of Matteo Contarelli, and indeed became a cardinal here in Rome before he died. He had left money for his chapel to be decorated, and Cesari had originally been given the job, but either out of laziness or of business elsewhere, I know not, he had not done it, and later had to return the fee.

So much, so boring.

Del Monte got me the commission. I don't know the backstage machinations, but he got it, and it was a bigger set of paintings than I had ever done, more than twice the size of any previous canvas, and it was also my first piece of history and big composition with several figures, and also my first public commission, and the public would be able to see it, and . . . and . . . I was so excited I can scarce get it all out. And . . . ?

It was mine.

There were to be two canvases, and both to illustrate some aspect of the apostle Matthew's life.

I did *The Calling of St Matthew* first, and it was a walk through.

For Matthew, when he was just still Levi the tax collector, I used a chap I had found with a beard. He is sitting at the table counting his taxes with a few of his drinking friends, including Minitti, looking very much the thing with some brand-new clothes, and another fellow in tights with my sword, the one I had given Fillide as a prop for her St Catherine. All that was just so, and I was very pleased. The table was on the left of the canvas, and the light source was high up and giving a slant of light as usual. And then I painted Our Lord on the right, as if he had just come in out of the cold and is beckoning Levi to follow.

And by Christ he looked awful. Just like a sack of flour dumped in the corner, with his stupid nightdress instead of proper clothes and an expression of sickening piety. How can you get around all that? It is all specified in the Church's instructions to painters, written quite clearly. But there is no way in this world that you can make holiness look interesting. You want to dig him in the ribs, or point at him and laugh. He killed the painting stone dead.

So I painted Peter in front of him, fussing about doing something obscure, maybe ticking off one of the *bravi* at the table. Actually Peter's line of sight is a bit off kilter. Where he is looking is a bit indeterminate, but that doesn't matter because he is only there to obscure Christ. And he does it beautifully. All you can see now of Jesus is a rather stern jaw-line and nose, lit from behind, the light just barely scraping his cheek, and his beckoning finger, which I also changed so that it is hooked downwards. Some critic later said that I had copied it from Michelangelo's ceiling, the creation part, where God and Adam's fingers nearly connect, but that just shows what critics know.

The beckoning with a downward finger is simply how the Greeks do the act, I have seen it many times, and find it rather charming. Sometimes they use all their fingers, when they motion you to approach, and it is much less arrogant than the upwardly crooked finger.

I was worried what the clerics would say about my obscured Christ.

Not one word, is the answer to that. I don't think any of them even noticed. So much for devotional painting.

As usual I painted it fast, and with no preliminary drawing, and got it done in a few days, which pleased everyone all round, considering how long it had all been delayed. And I was mighty pleased with myself, with good reason I think. At last I was getting the fame that was my due. People will talk.

And I finished by leaving the table without a leg. I know it looks odd, but there were just too many human legs already under it, it would have got in the way, and anyway again I wondered how many people would notice. Again not a word. Well, it was dark in that corner of the chapel, it's true.

So I wiped my brushes and bundled them up and told the labourers how to hang it, and went for a drink in the Tavern of the Wolf as usual, and saw Fillide again, and pinched her arse, and she swore at me, and cuffed my ear. Which was nice.

And on my way home, I went through the Campo dei Fiori. And, O dear God help me, what I saw there!

It was late and the torches which the grooms and footmen leave in their holders around the place had been extinguished, so the square was dark and deserted. And in one corner there was a large pyre, with a stake in its middle, of the kind that Rome has seen too often lately. And a shady group of men in monks' robes busied themselves about the base of the pyre, lighting it from tapers which glimmered in the dark like glow-worms. And the kindling caught, and then the fire built up, quite quick, I think they must have put oil on it to help it catch speedily. And only then did I see the wretch who was tied to the stake. He was small and naked and his mouth had been cruelly gagged with a splintered piece of wood tied behind his head with a leather thong. He was signalling wildly through the flames, and his mouth was working like a furious horse's against the bridle. And one of the monks waved a crucifix on a long pole at him, but he averted his gaze and looked disgusted.

And then the flames began to take effect. Usually on

these occasions, one of the kindlier executioners (oh, they do exist) grants the condemned man the courtesy of strangulation, before lighting the bonfire. Or if not, the fumes and the smoke from the kindling leave the man unconscious, perhaps even dead, quite quick, so he is spared the torment of the flames. Not this time, though. The wretch's skin began to turn black and blisters burst all over him and strips of skin began to fall from his scorched body, and all the while he was writhing and battling against his bonds. His face was staring and his eyes near started from their sockets and he was screaming so loud over the flames that he could be heard the full length of the square, gag or no. But they were not screams of fear or agony. He was still shouting words at the top of his voice, still debating, still preaching for anyone with ears to hear. God alone would hear those words. God help him.

It was my friend Bruno.

I watched until he was silent. He just hung there burning. A man on fire, for all the world, I will swear he was an angel. The fire burned for three more hours before it was no more than embers. His bones still hung there on the blackened post, charred but unmistakable in the shape of a man.

A man burned to a shadow.

I watched and watched and only at the end did I notice the time. I did not weep, I never weep. Nor did I feel much finally. People often do talk of the shock of a fright, the shock which leaves a man dazed and dry-mouthed and glassy-eyed, and which may leave him close to death. I felt none of that. My eyes were dry, my heart beat slowly, my pulse was funereal, and my blood flowed quite sluggish through my body. I did not feel any rising in my gorge, nor the pressures on my brain which I admit does sometimes presage a rage in me. I was altogether quite steady and amazed only at my steadiness. Only one thing lived in my heart, and it was cold as a spike of ice. I would be avenged upon them all, the whole pack, every man jack.

The priests of the Inquisition would one day pay, I swore it. Bruno never harmed another man in his life, and his only great delight was in debating. But it was his downfall too, for the priests think there are some things which cannot be debated. So they did for him. Did the Pope know of this? You might as well ask: does he hate a Jew? No one can be burned without the Pope's say so. Would that the priesthood had but one neck, that I could feel it under my heel.

And the Pope? Something more slow for him, I think. Like an eternity spent in passing a stone, or years being devoured by scorpions, here under my eyes, where I can see him hurting. And that hook-nosed Jesuit bastard Bellarmino with him. Hell, it might even make me smile.

And no one ever saw me smile.

St Matthew

'. . . but stand
As if a man were author of himself
And knew no other kin.'

Shakespeare. *Coriolanus*

I lied to you earlier when I said that *The Calling of St Matthew* was my first of the two paintings commissioned for the Contarelli chapel. It was not. I worked on *The Martyrdom of St Matthew* before it. I am sorry. Not that I care about lying one way or the other. I will lie to anyone, provided they deserve it. But it is just that I have kept up the pretence so long now that it has become a virtual truth for me. I have forgotten the key sequence of events. But the truth is that I began *The Martyrdom* and got it all hopelessly wrong. And that is something I did not like to admit to at the time. And I persisted in the lie so long that correcting it became too bothersome.

It was the only time in my life that I have blundered badly in a painting and I am still not sure exactly what I did wrong. Many things probably, or rather I think it was a sequence of false steps, by which one *malpasso* leads to another.

First, I paid too much attention to what old Contarelli had asked for in the composition. There was a lot of nonsense about an altar and steps up to it, with the already wounded saint on the altar steps, and then a congregation of the faithful standing around looking pious and saying, 'Oh look, another martyrdom, let's go dip our fingers in the blood and store up a bit of goodness for when we die.'

The thing about patrons is that they really have not got a clue as to what they want, and it's your business to show them, to give them not what they think they want, but what they really need. Give them what they truly need and deserve and all thought of what they originally asked for will fly out of their head. I guarantee it. You could ask a hundred men in the street how to improve the city, and they will all say, better lighting, sweeter water from the wells, firmer paving in the piazzas and so on forever, but what they really want, what they really spend their money on, is more taverns with more whores in them. Never trust an answer to a question that's put in public. You can always answer any question yourself. Just look inwardly and be honest, with yourself at least if no one else.

Where was I? Oh yes, he wanted some sort of altar, and so God rot me for ever being so stupid, I started painting a whacking great edifice with classical pillars and steps and columns and pitched roofs and Lord knows what else besides. I simply do not know where it came from, for, while I can paint a good likeness, I have absolutely no interest in doing buildings whatsoever. A few stones here or there and a window or two are all I ever need to set a scene. Let masons and architects draw up plans for their bits of stone, and square and hew green trees till the forests are bare. I'll none of it.

And not content with messing around with a huge, great lump of a building I then started putting in the figures as Contarelli wanted them. It's not as if he had been breathing down my neck. Christ, he was already dead and buried, and I have no false piety concerning the wishes of the dead, let them rot with their owner. But still I persisted in the stupid course.

Perhaps it was the burning of Bruno that undid me. My mind was not settled for a long time after, and I brooded much upon the poor man and his fate. St Matthew was not burned, but stabbed by some thug with a sword. Still, there was violence in my mind and I used it.

And before long I knew that it just would not do. It was a bastard thing, which owed much to following the injunctions of others and, even worse, following the style of certain local painters, which I always knew to be a dead end. Above all, it owed nothing to life. Somewhere along the line I had forgotten my vow, to only ever take my paintings straight from life.

So I stopped doing what I was doing there, went out, got roaring drunk, had a whore, came back and got started on the other painting before the hangover even set in. Got it done in record time too. The one about Matthew's Calling, I told you about before. I'm proud of that one, and like it much whenever I recall it, because it was the one painting that got me back on my tracks. And I like the nicely turned thighs and calves that I gave to Minitti under the table. He's got a good pair of pins there, that boy.

Anyway it restored my confidence and I returned to the Martyrdom, which I had scrubbed over with burnt sienna in disgust, and got cracking again on that, and that was soon my best picture to date. It was also the largest and had a good thirteen men in it. No women either.

Matthew is at the centre, as you can obviously see, but what is new is the way I arranged all the onlookers. They spring outwards from the bloody deed all in different directions, so that they form a pattern rather like the spokes of a wheel, flying out from the hub. Painters before me usually have worked in triangles and diagonals. This was different, and I was finally pleased. There is a pretty boy turning away on the right and screaming at the outrage. Others too are in some horror. There is an angel descending with the martyr's palm branch, which is a bit before the fact, I think, but will please the priests.

And in the background you will see an ugly, bearded face, passing the scene, and looking on with some dismay, but staring and staring with an unblinking snake's eye. And passing by on the other side.

That's me.

I like putting myself in my paintings, on the sidelines as it were. It's better than a signature, which some men affect. And it says, 'I was there. I looked at this and this is how it was, as close to life as I can get it.' True, I look a bit ill, but this malaria is plaguing me again. And poor little Bruno too, I can't get his burning out of my mind. I sleep little, and always dream of those flames, and his charred skin.

So there it is, my first two great public pieces, and only now, late in life, can I admit that I lost my nerve over one of them. It was the burning of Bruno, it was the instructions from Contarelli, it was my desire to please others, it was a distrust of the new Pope's fig-leaf laws, it was . . . I could find you a hundred more reasons, but I shall not. The error was in me, solely in me, and never again would I allow myself to fall for it.

I will paint only in the way I have chosen. I will not draw, and I will take straight from life, and render it true in colour. You think that that is not very much, perhaps. Look around at my contemporaries, then. They gave up looking at life a long time ago and just do writhing rag dolls with luminous skin instead, which comes from nothing but other paintings and what's in their minds. Damn their pious ideals. If my saint has dirt under his fingernails, so be it. If my executioner has grimy soles to his feet, then he will have them in the picture. It's life for me.

Peter and Paul

Beware of all enterprises that require new clothes

Henry David Thoreau. *Walden. (1854)*

After that I found fame. They came from all around to look and wonder. And none of them realized that I had done something new. It was too new for them to see it. One fool, who actually wrote about it later, thought that the executioner in the Martyrdom must be a figure of Christ, throwing the moneylenders out of the temple. Critics, what can you do about them? What a shower of shit. Each thinks that he has some claim to the painting, and that only he can truly understand it.

Fame I did not care for much, but it brought more work as it will. Fate goes where fate must. No one gives you work when you are out of work and need it most. Find yourself in work, though, and the offers come pouring in.

Cerasi offered me a good price (so he bloody should; he's only the Pope's treasurer) for a pair of new paintings for his chapel he had just bought on S. Maria del Popolo. It was a damp place so I decided to do them on wood that had been properly prepared. I did a *Crucifixion of St Peter*, which did away with soaring heavenly hosts and all that baggage and just concentrated on a baffled and horrified old man being hoisted into position, upside down you will recall, by three dirty labourers. Space in the chapel was tight and so I crowded the figures right to the edge of the frame. And the picture was hung in an odd place, so that the angle of viewing was a bit skewed. This meant that the main thing sticking in the viewers' face was an executioner's huge arse. That was no accident on my part. None of the priests mentioned it; but many who came to see it quietly laughed behind their hands.

And it gave me an idea for the other painting, which was to be a *Conversion of St Paul on the Road to Damascus*. You will remember the story: Saul on the road, bright light from heaven, thunderous voice, kicking against the pricks, the man falls off horse, blinded for three days, wakes up a Christian and becomes St Paul.

As far as biblical stories go: there is hot runny crap, and there is hard constipated crap. This strikes me as the hot runny kind; squits, runs, dysentery. Look at St Paul. Was there ever a more disastrous sort of figure in the history of any religion? Even Mohammed is a merciful man by comparison.

Anyway, I knew that Cerasi had also commissioned a picture for the chapel from Hannibal Caracci, the cunning bugger. For Caracci was my only rival in Rome since my

Matthew paintings. So there was Cerasi quietly rubbing his hands together over a sort of painting horserace, with me and Caracci on the starting line, side by side, and all of Rome coming to compare us and judge between my *St Paul* and his *Assumption*. Well to hell with that idea, I'm not competing with any other dauber, no matter that he be ten years my senior. No matter that I quite like him and hold his works to be good.

As a matter of fact I had already done one *Conversion of St Paul*. It was a piece of hackwork and pretty crappy hackwork at that. Bearded men in silly hats, angels plummeting from heaven, rearing horse, that sort of thing. You can't do a rearing horse from life, can you? That much is bleeding obvious just by looking at every painting of a rearing horse in existence. They all look as stiff as a child's rocking horse. Which of course is not surprising, since that is exactly what they were painted from. So, I got hold of a horse. Not just any horse, but a real old dobbin.

Now St Paul is usually depicted dropping off a rearing Arab stallion of impeccable pedigree. But not my St Paul. All he could afford was this knock-kneed nag, with a back like a hammock and hooves as big as dinner plates. And I lugged horsey all the way up into the studio and had him pose, sweating with the heat and dribbling a bit onto the floor. He was so old, he gave me no trouble about standing still. I just hired an old dotard to hold his muzzle and give him oats occasionally. And I put him clear across the whole painting, so that Paul is overshadowed by this enormous mournful old nag. And best of all, when hung next to Caracci's smug little Virgin swimming up to heaven surrounded by hundreds of swooning sycophants, what draws the eye away from his tooth-rotting confection is my enormous horse's enormous arse.

I win.

Cerasi paid me 400 *scudi*. Good money in those days.

I bought a new black suit, velvet this time, of better quality than the last, which was getting a bit ragged now after three years of continuous wearing. Dropped the old one on a rubbish heap and also acquired a boy servant, who could at least carry my sword for me at night. I had been arrested not long before for carrying a weapon, and the bastards kept me in overnight, in spite of me insisting I was a member of del Monte's household. The idiot *sbirri* had never heard of him. Really, you do find a poor quality of policeman these days. So for the foreseeable future I can at least venture out with my weapon, in search of mayhem. I have been working too hard lately and I need some fun. The boy is sweet. Ah, mischief.

Went out that very night of finishing. Saw that waiter into whose face I had once thrown a plate of artichokes (I forgot to tell you about that – nothing to it really, he was just a bit cheeky). He's still got the scar on his cheek, as a matter of fact, and he cringes slightly when he first sees me, before putting on his best front and ostentatiously refusing to serve me. I'll fuck him one day, teach him a lesson. Till then, I was happy to see Minitti and Longhi and the boys. Minitti was subdued, as he always seems to be these days. He is talking about getting married so I guess he is reaching that stage of boredom which spells the end of originality in a man. I can see it on him, like a sodden cloak in a rainstorm. He will wed some wide-hipped sow, and she'll produce five squalling brats, and he will get broad across the beam, like a castrato, which is roughly what he will become anyway, and his paintings will be shot to shit.

Greatness is given to few, and believe me I would never condemn the man who chooses not to tread that hard and lonely path. If I could do otherwise, believe me I would. But I cannot, I am not driven, but called. And I have not Odysseus's strength of character who, when he heard the Sirens' call, plugged up his men's ears and bound himself to the mast. I just follow the call.

So no more brawling for Minitti. Fair enough. He has a lovely rounded, chubby-cheeked face, and I would not wish it scarred. Myself, I start at a disadvantage. The only thing scars can do for me is make my face even more sinister. If your face is going to frighten children, then you might as well scare them to death. So a few more scars, then, before I die.

I almost said before I retire and settle down. Christ, what is coming over me? My knees may creak a bit these days, and my liver gives me hell when I drink, after all that malaria. But Jesus, settle down? I'd sooner stick hot irons in my eyes.

The Taking of Christ

If we do not find anything pleasant, at least we shall find something new.

Voltaire. *Candide. 1759*

I spent a year or so doing nothing but paint. That sounds unlike me, I know, but there it was, I do not know why the roaring in me calmed, but it did. I did a lot of stuff for Cardinal Mattei, and I could tell you all about him, but I won't, for you would drop down dead from boredom before I had finished my first sentence. There was just nothing to him worth describing, and I did a *St John*, and another *St John in the Wilderness*, and *Christ's Supper at Emmaus*, and a great *Doubting Thomas*, which has an ancient creaking bent-double Thomas sticking his finger in Christ's wound and opening up the slit in a way which is frankly sexual, although needless to say everyone kept their mouth shut on that score. And a whole load of other stuff I can't be bothered to go into right now, I am thirty-nine years old and life is getting too short for all the details.

Perhaps I'll do a calm painting sometime. I never have so far.

But one pleased me greatly. I think it one of my best, or at least the one with the most action in it. It is my *Taking of Christ, in the Garden of Gethsemane.* The whole thing is crammed with people right to the edge of the frame, and there is so much bustling about that their limbs are confused, almost intertwined. There is a disgusting looking Judas, grabbing Jesus by the arm and planting a lewd great kiss on his cheek, which looks very ambiguous. And there is Christ looking revoltingly penitential as usual, all pious finger-folding and downcast gaze and humble acceptance of his fate, the stupid weedy boy. And there's a fleeing disciple, and various onlookers, including me at the back lifting a lantern and trying to shed some light on the dark.

But the best thing is my soldier in black armour. I knew I would use that black armour I saw in Venice one day. He is looming right over the whole picture, in the foreground, with his arm outstretched right across to Christ. That mighty arm, I tell you, it breaks all the rules in the book. It goes right the way across the front of the picture, and bars the viewer from entry into the action, almost bars him from looking at it at all. And the light glints off that arm and it is so deep a black as to be the armour of the devil himself. It's a beauty, and I was well pleased for I had broken fresh ground and done something new.

No one noticed. It just hung there, adorning the wall. I sometimes think I should have gone into designing wallpaper. Perhaps I have.

Defamation and Prison

The greater the truth, the greater the libel

Proverb, eighteenth century

That fool Baglione was the beginning of my undoing. He had gotten a commission from the Jesuits to do a painting for one of their cesspit churches. God rot the whole fusty stinking pack of them. They were the only order who never gave me a commission, and they claimed it was because of the profane and ignoble elements in my paintings. But the whole world knew perfectly well it was because I openly detested them and their ways. Just when the Church was failing and near to dying in most people's eyes, and the Protestants in the north were holding all the cards, along came the Jesuits with their insinuations and their stress on the confessional as the foundation stone on which to build their stinking edifice of Catholic orthodoxy.

I went to see Baglione's finished painting, a 'Resurrection' in the Gesu, with Longhi and with the painter Orazio Gentileschi and also with Trisegni, all friends of mine or at least men I got on with tolerably well, or at least had no immediate objection to. They knew what to wear and what to say, and they were easy with me, which God knows is hard enough for most men.

It was terrible. It was unveiled on an Easter Sunday, and if it wasn't the worst painting I had ever seen, it was damn close to it. Christ rising was the usual pious crap done in the style of *la manière*, which should be dead soon with any luck, if I have my way. Anyway there we were the three of us, staring at this thing there with our jaws slack in amazement. Nobody could think of anything to say, indeed words seemed superfluous. Gentileschi started it all by laughing, and pretty soon Longhi and I got infected and by then we were all but rolling in the aisles at this bloated piece of confectionary. Our mockery stopped some of the worshippers in their tracks and earned us very dirty looks from the priests, even though there was no service under way.

We staggered out of the church, and slowly calmed down, and then Longhi gave me a look, which made me know exactly what was on his mind. Here was this fool Baglione, by any standards an affront to anyone with half a brain cell, and he was *alive and walking the streets.*

Longhi looked at me long and hard outside that church with something like a smile at the corners of his mouth and I knew he was plotting something for us to do.

Anyway we went back in and started talking loudly off the tops of our heads about what a terrible piece of daubing it all was, and how he had got all the colours wrong and he could not do a perspective to save his life, and how derivative it all was.

And there I noticed in one corner was that little weasel Mao Salini. He had hopes of being a painter and had clung to Baglione's shirt-tails all these years, even when everyone else had deserted the man for his faults. What a born loser that Mao was. I almost felt sorry for the twisted little boy. The trouble was that I had already hit the little bastard once or twice before, for no real reason other than he was an offence to the eye.

Christ, he was an offence to all creation. He was a walking proof that God put miscarriage on this earth for a reason.

And he had complained to the authorities about me and had even had me hauled up before the bench before I was famous enough to get away with it. So I could see he was still festering away with ancient grievances. And here we were laughing at his wretched master's masterwork.

He took off like a rat with a flaming torch stuffed up its arse. And I knew exactly where he was off to, but what they would devise I wasn't sure.

It hit us a couple of months later, having been carefully plotted out in some detail. The *sbirri* came for me after lunch one day at the Palazzo Madama, and poor old Cardinal del Monte got another nasty shock from my life, poor chap. He was dithering around pulling on his beard and going oh dear oh dear what can I do, call my lawyers. There was nothing to be done about it. Just another bad day that I had given my patron, in a long list of bad days. Poor man, he did love me so, and he suffered for it.

In prison they read me the charges of criminal libel. Pretty soon, within a day or two, Gentileschi and Trisegni joined me, although Longhi, the crafty bastard, was out of town, so no one could get at him.

It seems that Baglione had accused us of circulating various obscene poems about him and his dirty habits. One was called 'Giovan Coglione', or 'John Cock', it names the painter as a giant prick and makes it pretty clear he doesn't deserve the honours heaped upon him. There was another too, called 'Giovan Bagaglia', or 'John Baggage', which suggested that he take all his paintings and either wipe his arse with them or stuff them up Mao's wife's cunt, since he was no longer fucking that.

My, such language!

There was whole lot of other stuff too, about how all of this had sprung from my jealousy because I wanted the commission from the Jesuits to do the painting, which any fool would know was crap because I have never been commissioned from the Jesuits, nor ever likely to be neither. It was heavyweight stuff, though; libel could carry a death penalty if bad enough and this was bad.

What was worse, Mao, who had run to the police waving these poems above his head and snivelling about it all, also said somewhere in the deposition that the three of us had got it all together with the aid of Minitti and 'Caravaggio's fuck boy' called 'Batista, who lives at the Banchi'. Now that was nasty. I could hang for that. Though I thought I would not, because it is very, very rare for anyone to make that kind of statement in the open. If they do and it is not proved, they could be hanged themselves for such a slander. Mao had no proof I had been doing Batista, I was pretty sure of that.

As to the other thing, what to do? I was unsure to start with, but a day or two in prison, with the shadow of the noose falling across your bench, concentrates the mind wonderfully.

The thing was: I had hardly stepped fully into my new role as Rome's best painter. It was one thing to know it from a very early age even before you had got started, but quite another to live up to it, once your audience had confirmed you in the role. But that is what I had become; it is what I was. Time to adopt a few airs and graces. Time to scare up a little respect. There was only one thing to do here, I realized. Brass it out.

Trisegni dithered around a bit, accusing Mao of lying, which of course just set up a tit for tat of 'No, you're lying,' 'No, you're lying' between them and left the court and judges exasperated. That was going nowhere, and things were not looking happy. The police had searched Gentileschi's house and also Longhi's and had found a few similar poems, but nothing libellous.

I took the stand, looking thoughtful, bold and haughty.

I had seen enough actors in my time to know what to do. Breathe slowly, enunciate clearly, look upwards and to the right, you'll have them in your palm soon enough.

They began by questioning me about painters, the fools. I can run rings around them on that point. I could see why, too; they were trying to establish jealousy as a motive for my libel. Well, I would give them just enough truth so that they could not catch me out on anything, but no more truth than was necessary. That much I have learnt from our Jesuit brethren.

They asked me what painters I knew in Rome. Strange beginning, but I let them have it. I rather liked the list of people I spelled out for them. It has a ring to it. Try saying it out loud:

Giovanni Baglione
Annibale Carracci
Guiseppe Cesari
Cavaliere d'Arpino
Giovanni Andrea Donducci, known as il Mastelletta
Orazio Gentileschi
Gismondo Laer
Prospero Orsi
Pomarancio
Roncalli
Antonio Tempesta
Giorgio Todesco
Federico Zuccaro

A pretty good line-up, I think you will agree, and me rather like a major-domo announcing the guests at a grand function for all the best artists. I named them in alphabetical order rather than order of merit, although it was clear that the dolts on the bench hadn't heard of half of them. So I added that while most of them were known to me, some were my friends, but not all of them were good men. They seized on that pretty quick, as I knew they would. How would I define 'good men', they said, as if they had never heard of one before.

I stroked my beard and was silent as if in thought for a moment or two, though in truth I knew already what I was going to say.

'A *valent'uomo*, by which I mean a good man, is, for me at any rate, someone who knows how to do things well, that is, he who knows how to do well by his craft. That may not sound like much, but how many men do anything truly well? I refer in this case of course to artists. So, in painting, a *valent'uomo* knows how to paint well and how to imitate natural objects well.' I emphasized the last phrase but I am sure they hadn't a clue as to what I was talking about. Besides, I was laying on the sarcasm a bit thick. So they swerved back to naming names. They wanted to know which of the painters were my enemies.

I told them that d'Arpino, Baglione, Gentileschi and Todesco were not friends of mine because we did not speak to each other any more. It was a bit of a risk naming

Gentileschi, because I had been speaking to him quite recently, but to link my co-defendant with my accuser was a good move, I thought.

Then they asked me straight out whether I ever wrote poetry. After stroking my beard for a while, and staring into space, I said that I would like to revise my list of painters. I would say that only four are of major importance, and they would be: d'Arpino, Roncalli, Carracci, and Zuccaro. Oh, and maybe Tempesta. That's it.

They didn't notice I had changed the subject. Anyway, everything I said was pure smokescreen. Sometimes I think investigative magistrates are as stupid as a bag of hammers.

Finally they asked me what I thought of Baglione as a painter, and I could not bring myself to lie about that, even though it would have been best for me. I had anticipated this question and I wondered whether I could get away with damning with faint praise. Then I thought fuck all that, let them have both barrels. At least it strengthens my claims to honesty. A less honest man would have claimed to quite like Baglione or some such piece of soft soap.

I told them that I had seen his *Resurrection* and it was a clumsy piece. They perked up a bit at that, I can tell you, so I went in blazing. I said that moreover I didn't know of a single other painter who liked the picture. And what's more, I didn't know of a single other painter who thought Baglione was any kind of good painter. Christ, that put the rats up their trouser legs. Two of them were positively gobbling with indignation.

And it was then I saw the hand of the Jesuits behind all this. If you condemn Baglione as a painter, then you condemn the taste of the Jesuits who commissioned and approved of him. Whoops. And you condemn the whole of the bloody counter-Reformation and the whole rat-bastard boiling lot of them. I would not be at all surprised if the Jesuits weren't behind this whole bleeding trial. Just to do me in.

Where the hell is Longhi? I wish he were here. He'd run the lot of them through with his dagger and have done with it. I'm worried. Worried? Fuck me, if I wasn't putting on a good front, I'd be shitting in my breeches. Good job they're black.

And so I laid in finally with a blow at Mao. Hung for a sheep, I thought. No one praises Baglione, I repeated, unless it be that guy who follows him around like a guardian angel. I used the phrase guardian angel, but I put the emphasis on angel, and I think they caught my drift. Mao was Baggy's bum boy, was what I was suggesting. There was a certain amount of coughing and shuffling and harrumphing after that. There was altogether too much accusation of sodomy flying around in the air for their Excellencies' comfort. No one likes to mention it, let alone ask for proof. There is just too much at stake for everyone. Better by far to put it down to common abuse in the midst of an affray. Idle words, too much drink, high-spirited insult – that sort of thing. We're talking burning here.

So I climbed back up to the exalted level I had taken on in my role as Rome's greatest painter. And I fixed them with a steady gaze and puffed out my chest and told them that I had never heard or read anything written, either in Latin or our language, which even mentioned Baglione, let alone libelled him. Or indeed little Mao. And with that I swept off in disdain, as far as that was possible with jailers in attendance.

I can cut a dash with the best of them. And I can scare men too. No need for any of the vulgar language in the poems; and I had marginalized Baglione completely as a woeful second-rater.

The case remained unproved for a little while longer, while they made pretence of trying to find Longhi for interrogation, but the outcome was already known around Rome. Baglione did not have a leg to stand on. It was only a question of time before I was released and he was a common laughing stock.

So we did well to write those poems, Longhi and I.

Sprung by the Frog

Ten days later and I was still lying around in the lockup. It could only be the Jesuits operating behind the scenes, working up something to nail us on, I am sure of it.

And I was looking out the barred window one sunny morning and what did I see but Philipe de Béthune striding firmly across the stones of the courtyard, his cloak snapping in the breeze like a proud flag, as if he was on a mission from God. Which, as far as I was concerned, was exactly what it turned out to be. Béthune may be very tall, and uncommonly full of himself, but he is a truly impressive figure for the simple reason he knows exactly how to tell men to do things. When he tells you to do something, you get it done. I could hear him raise his voice just once in the distant offices of the jail. 'Don't be a cunt, man,' he bellowed. And after that there was a pallid silence of a few moments and then I heard the blessed clinking of keys on a ring and my door was opened by a sheepish jailer.

And we walked back together the way he had come across the courtyard and I never liked a man so much in my life before. No wonder he was the French Ambassador to Rome. And then comes the big question into my mind: so why had he come for me?

He sensed that question even as it formed in my mind. 'We liked the pictures you did for our church . . .' he said, in an offhand sort of way while scanning the horizon as if expecting to see something approaching from the distance, like a flock of auspicious birds or a squadron of Hun cavalry. He was referring to my St Matthew pictures in the Church of Saint Louis for the French.

'And I liked that Danae you did for me, all those naked female breasts and bottoms, lovely, lovely, I have to keep it behind a little green curtain, wouldn't want to frighten the servants, or me wife, come to that. I unveil it after dinner, when we are all smoking, keeps me friends and colleagues very happy.' He chortled happily. And then he slipped in, almost as an afterthought, the way these people do when they want to say something important: 'And we hate the Jesuits like poison,' slightly more sotto voce than before, though not by much. 'Barberini asked me to come, sort out this silly business,' he said by way of putting an end to the whole subject. Where do types like him get it from, this *sprezzatura*, I wonder? And can I have it too? A knighthood would be as good a place to start as any.

Barberini was a cardinal. I had been doing an 'Abraham and Isaac' for him. Nice man, sweet face, crafty as a snake, not a Jesuit, rich, and he could be Pope one day. My kind of man.

The French were always suspicious of this new-made faction. Henri of Navarre had gone Protestant for a while, but then there was all that stuff with the Huguenots getting massacred, and he had gone back to the bosom of the Pope purely for reasons of internal politics. The French were riven with factions. Not that the Pope believed him entirely. There were all sorts of interviews to ascertain his sincerity. And one of the key demands for being welcomed back into the fold was that he allow the Jesuits into his country.

'Not asking much, is it?' said the Pope.

'Only the death of every damn thing I like about this country and my life in it,' thought Henri to himself. So he stalled a while. Béthune was doing a grand job, keeping the Pope happy, while Henri dithered. I had seen the spy Vialardi coming and going from the Embassy too, so there were dark deeds afoot, you can be sure.

'Now you're out,' said Béthune, 'you can finish that Abraham thing for us, eh?' and smiled and patted my cheek and turned on his heel and was off, all in one seamless movement. As he walked away his head was lowered as if he was lost in thought. I noticed that people got out of his way as he approached, without even glancing at him. A brief fluttering swag of cloak as he turned the corner was my last sight of him. I must buy a new black cloak. And get back to my painting. Just a couple of days without a brush in my hand is too long. I get pangs, like hunger, if I neglect my art. Unless I'm drinking, or whoring, or fighting of course; then the world looks slightly better, and the pain goes away.

I said that once to Minitti and he asked me 'What pain?' with some sweet concern as if I were sick. 'The pain of being a man,' I said, and he looked baffled and I felt pompous. There we are. It's the best I can do.

So I finished the Abraham picture for Cardinal Maffeo Barberini, and a sick thing it was too, with the daft old man holding his son down by the throat in no uncertain terms and about to saw through his neck with a nasty looking blade, and, lo, an angel of the Lord appearing to stay his hand. Quite why the good and merciful Lord had demanded that the poor old bastard kill his son in the first place is one of the nastier of God's little jokes on mankind. If anyone demanded that I do that as a proof of my love for them I'd say: Fuck off, you sick bastard. But then Abraham does not strike me as one of life's brighter pennies.

I arranged it so that the painting was full of an ugly sort of violence. Far from being a sacrifice to the Lord, it looks more like an old man about to violate some poor country boy, and dispatch him with his knife after buggering him. The intervening angel had an absolutely dotty expression on his face, almost as if he'd like to join in. Let Barberini make of it as he likes.

After I was let out of prison, part of the legal order confined me to my house for a while and so I moved to a place not far from my stamping ground around the Piazza Navona. It was a well-built two-story house, with a room at street level large enough for my studio. I bought a bed and a chair and a table for my paints, and that was it. I can't abide furniture, and if anyone wants to visit they can stand or sit on the floor. No one stays for long, I can tell you, which is the way I like it. I hacked a hole in the studio's ceiling to the upper floor, through which I could project beams of light in the direction I wanted. I don't suppose the landlady will approve, but screw her.

Longhi got back from his travels and faced down snivelling Mao in church one day, calling him a snitch and a liar, and damn near killed him outside with his sword, but for the intervention of some passer-by who testified to it all later in court. Longhi vanished again. Sometimes I think he is almost as wicked as I. But he can't be because he does not frighten me.

Now that it comes to my mind, nobody does. At least, nobody yet in my life. Nor any thing. I should have known better than to tempt the gods.

The Dirty Streets of Loreto

Give me my scallop shell of quiet,
My staff of faith to walk upon,
My scrip of joy, immortal diet,
My bottle of salvation,
My gown of glory, hope's true gage,
And thus I'll take my pilgrimage

'Sir Walter Raleigh to the Queen' 1604

I did a *Madonna of Loreto*, and I used Fillide for it. Loreto was
the place outside Rome which contains the house where
Jesus was born.

Oh, ho, that pulled you up a bit short that didn't it? I
would bet good money you never knew about that one. Well,
while the rest of the world thought the stable was in
Bethlehem, we Romans know better. Apparently some
angels got together about a thousand years ago and realized
that what with Bethlehem being under the heel of the unholy
Arabs and Rome now being the centre of the civilized
Christian world, then they had better do something about the
birthplace of the Holy One. What they did was lift it up and

fly it, lock stock and barrel, all the way across the sea and drop it conveniently far enough outside Rome to make it a bit of a pilgrimage for the faithful to get there.

I went there once. It was a pretty empty sort of town, and the stable nothing much to get heated up about. But all through the day, hundreds and hundreds of idiot barefoot pilgrims all flocked to see it and grovel.

So that's what I painted. I mean, no flying barns or anything like that, not my style at all. There is quite enough of that devotional drivel cluttering up chapels all over the place as it is. No, I painted two humble men on their knees at the doorstep, their dirty feet all but thrusting out of the canvas and onto your nose. And at the door, leaning nonchalantly against the jamb, the Madonna holding up her infant for them. Not just any old Madonna either, I used Fillide in profile in a dark red dress. It was some time since I had used red in one of my paintings, and I think it may be the last. It is too disturbing a colour for what I need.

But she looks gorgeous. Not like a mother of a Lord, more like the doe-eyed seductress she was in real life. And I thought my putting someone that recognizable into the role of God's mother would get me into trouble, what with it being specifically forbidden in the Pope's Rulebook. Not a bit of it. What the priests didn't like this time were the pilgrims' dirty feet. 'Lowering the tone,' was the phrase they used I think, as if it was only the rich that ever went on pilgrimages. Or knew how to pray. I give up. I can annoy them all right, but I just can't seem to annoy them in the way that I want to. It won't do.

I was in trouble over Fillide again in no time at all. What is it about women? They come trailing clouds of trouble behind them. I was thinking of my next project and it was thinking of Fillide led me to it.

Ranuccio and Fillide

Anger and jealousy can no more bear to lose sight
of their subjects than love.

George Eliot. *The Mill on the Floss. 1860*

Ranuccio fell for her, the fool. He was ever as light as a woman in his love life. He paid for her, the same as any other man, to start with. But then he heard that Strozzi was her patron, and like as not to marry her, and he became jealous. Oh, how I love to see jealousy take its grip on a man. I have never understood it myself. Just once or twice in the past I have felt a pang, but it soon passes, thanks to drink, or a brawl, or better still when I am painting, for then I think of nothing else.

No woman is worth that much emotion, not when another is available. Only a fool would get that possessive over something he can replace so easily. Why spend good money on a book, when you can so easily borrow another man's? I feel the same about women.

But Ranuccio was caught by the green-eyed monster, and what a wonder he was to behold. It gripped him, and stretched him on its griddle, and there he seethed in its flames. He lost weight, and could not sleep so that he looked haggard, like a penitent forever scourging himself. And his temper became ever stretched till he burned on a short fuse. If God wanted to give His sinners a foretaste of hell, He surely invented jealousy and put it in men's hearts for that end. Why else is it here, on earth? I do not understand it.

For this was surely hell, and Ranuccio was in it. By day he moped and whined and could talk of nothing but the wretched woman. By night he drank and roared and picked fights he knew he would lose, the better to be shamed and humiliated. He would stand outside her house, not like a wooer under a balcony, but just to see if another man entered.

One man he saw, and thought he recognized and went to strike him down, before a friend held him back and reminded him it was Fillide's brother come to visit. So blinded was he by this monster. He was hauled twice before the magistrates for throwing stones at her window. The second time, it was actually me who had thrown them. I knew they would arrest him, and could not resist the joke. He was told of it, later, by others, but he never reproached me. He knew what a fool he looked, and he wanted punishment. But it could not stop him, however bitter the taste of public approbation. He went half mad, though the moon was nowhere near full. And, strangely, people understood, and were kind, and let him go his ways, thinking perhaps it would pass. It did not.

Several times he called at the Strozzi Palace on spurious business of one kind or another, and, I was told, would linger in the hall, where he could gaze on my portrait of Fillide. Meanwhile, what he did not know, I was painting her again, this time in something more provocative. She had been mine in the flesh, now she was mine on canvas. And he had been mine too, bodily, as I have described. But now he was mine in spirit, and evil is so much more spiritually attractive than good, don't you think? Now I possessed him more totally than when I fucked him. And I wanted him to wriggle on the end of my hook like a codfish.

He heard she was modelling for me again. And he hung around my studio, waiting for her, and would interrogate her at the end of the day about the painting and what we were up to. She told him nothing. I had told her nothing of my little games with him, but sometimes I think she was in it all deeper than I. Women can sniff these things, and their cruelty is more refined than men's.

A Duel

We must have bloody noses and cracked crowns.

Shakespeare. *Henry IV Part I. 1597*

I killed him on a Sunday afternoon late into May. The weather was vile, hot and shiny as molten brass, with livid clouds close-packed and hanging above the rooftops, crowding down and threatening rain later. The mood in the streets was palpable. There had been rumours of a war with Venice, and they still had not yet abated. Venice was ever a thorn in the side of the Spanish, who wanted to extend their control over all of this country, they were so greedy. They had been mobilizing their troops through Lombardy and rattling their sabres, clearing their throats and spitting in the general direction of La Serenissima.

But Venice wasn't so easily unseated. Its glory days may be over, but it is still rich, and powerful and jealous of its Republican isolation. And hard to get to, what with all that water and putrid swamp between it and its would-be conquerers. And it had the French on its side, which is why it had been so close to Protestantism for a while.

It sent out no envoys, no messages pleading for peace, nor anything at all. Just sat there waiting, quietly sucking its thumb and laughing up its sleeve, and that unnerved the Spanish more than anything. Venice wasn't for burning, oh no.

The papal troops were ordered back to their barracks and Rome was bulging with them all. The place was seething with disgruntled soldiers, all geared up for a fight and nowhere to take it. The place was fair reeking of manhood, and the whores were getting such a good seeing-to of an evening that they forgot to charge after a while.

There had been some sort of celebration with fireworks, an anniversary I think, probably the birthday of one of the Pope's children. And all of Rome had been out on the streets, although the mood was volatile and there had ugly incidents here and there. There had been much chanting against the Spanish. It may have been incited by the pro-Frenchies, but I don't think so. The ignorant populace is far more inclined in its ways and thinking toward the French. They know them well enough and like what they see: a cultivated lot of men, who may well be in it for what they can get out of it, but at least treat the locals well. Unlike the Spanish, who steal your bread, and then the flour that you made it from, and then the wheat even from the silo, and then grind your face in the dust that's left on the floor.

Anyway, the weather and the atmosphere were both heavy

with menace, and men such as I are much influenced by both I think. Even the moon can have an effect upon me.

That Sunday afternoon, I drifted towards the tennis courts, which were still out on the Campo Marzio, close by where I used to live at del Monte's palazzo. I was happy because that morning I had come around a corner and seen a wonderful sight.

A mob were putting the finishing touches to beating up Bellarmino's retinue. Oh, what a heavenly vision. They had set upon the procession and dragged the cardinal from his carriage and spat on him and kicked him into the dust, and left it at that because if they had harmed him more or even killed him then heads would have rolled. But they could have a go at the column of guards with fair impunity, and so that is what they did. When I arrived it was all over, with about twenty-five men sitting or lying in the dust, cradling their heads and moaning a lot. There hadn't been naked steel here, only cudgels, for the mob were a wise lot. No killings, only broken heads, but it was enough to humiliate that hook-nosed bastard Jesuit, who killed the Cenci and my friend Bruno. He was staggering around his carriage, looking lost for once in his vainglorious life, and it gave me a great pleasure to point at him and sneer. I put my arm fully out and pointed and pointed and looked at him with such contempt that the crowd grew quite silent and like me just looked at him.

He nearly got back in his carriage, but realized that there

was no one to drive it. And so he was forced to walk through the mob, who would barely move out of his way, so that he was jostled and had a hard time of it getting through, cursing and swearing that we would all be punished for this. 'Punish just one of us, and the next time this happens, and it will be soon, I will kill you,' I said, not loudly, but loud enough to give him pause.

There was nothing the bastard could do, no witnesses of his nearby who could testify, no one he could suborn, so he pushed on. But not before he locked his gaze on me for more than a moment. He was memorizing my features, I could tell. Well, let him. He only has to set his secret service to work, and have them ask around the place about me. I am well enough known by now. But that look was nasty. It said, 'This is personal.'

That got my blood up, I can tell you. I could be burned for that. So I went to play tennis at the Pallacorda, in the Campo Marzio, where I believe they still have the courts to this day. And damn me if the matches weren't drawn up like battle with men arranged along French or Spanish lines. The mood was not good. Men were playing fit to bust, hammering the ball back over the net at top speed, and arguing the toss over line faults with the umpires. Large bets were being laid and boys running back and forth to the bookies with their masters' bets, money changing hands on the outcome of a set, and tempers were becoming ragged and hot. I loved it.

I took off my jacket and gave it to my boy with a coin and stepped into the French lines and went a few sets against a couple of the Spanish clan. Beat them too, hands down, which annoyed them and won me a bit more money that I had laid out secretly on myself with a bookie. I am quite good at the sport, being quick on my feet. I only bet against myself if I am going to throw the game.

I left the game quite soon, for as I said it was very hot, and I was feeling very uneasy still. Something was in the air and I could smell it. I have seen dogs go quiet and sniff the air and whine and look scared just twenty minutes before an earthquake. So it was with me that day.

I saw Vialardi hanging around on the edge of things. Why is it that I always seem to be writing that sentence? Vialardi is always hanging around on the edge of things. He reminds me of a newspaper man I once came across; a great one for tugging at sleeves and whispering in corners. Always Johnnie-on-the-make, always Johnnie Eager, plotting, planning, conniving, who is in, who is out. Nasty little rat, he was.

And I went to my boy to collect my jacket and my winnings, for he had laid the money for me with the bookie. He handed me my jacket, but kept my sword (good boy, I have taught you well) and then pointed across the way. And there was Ranuccio, the stupid cunt, taking money from my bookie and looking shifty. Vialardi had just been talking with all three and was moving off into the crowd, rather too rapidly for my liking. 'What?' I asked the boy. He just shook his head and shrugged and looked across at Ranuccio.

Ranuccio had a look on his face that was smug. Not exactly triumphant, he wasn't so far out of his jealous fits yet, but he definitely looked like he had something over on me. I could guess. He had got wind of my betting on myself. Not a heinous crime, and only a little unlawful. He could report me if he wanted, but I knew he would not, for the *sbirri* couldn't care less about betting. No, he would just take the money that was mine and walk with it. And then spend it under my nose at some tavern. And jeer about my cheating and my getting caught out and just deserts and so on.

Well fuck that.

I hailed him, till I had his attention. And I called him 'a pig-eyed sack of shit'.

It was nice phrase that, I had been working it up for some time, and now its hour had come around. And I watched his face turn pale with anger.

I have seen men go red and the veins in their forehead begin to swell and pulse as if the blood might burst them open. But never before did I see a man go pale with rage. And for the first time in my life, I felt a pang of mortal fear. And I felt for my knife beneath my shirt, and he saw the move and turned and walked away with his head down, talking to himself, quite loudly, though none could make out the words. I knew then that it would end badly. But did I stop? Did I fuck.

I knew what to do next. It struck me with such clarity that there was no time between the thought and the action. I laughed at him, quite low, but clearly, so that he and other men might hear. It was no strategy. The laugh came upon me and I could not stop it, for I suddenly did indeed find it all very funny. It was the first time in my whole life that I laughed so, without bitterness. And the last.

He charged at me at full tilt, and boy could he run. He got off his heels like a rocket and was at top speed in just two steps, and by another five he was on me. Any other man would have borne the full brunt in a tumble and thrashed around as best they could. But Ranuccio, poor silly boy, had forgotten about me, or rather forgotten what I could do in a brawl. Unlike his brothers he was as yet untried in war, and truth to tell I do not think he would ever last long as a soldier. I mean, God, he had known me well enough, known what I was like, I had even fucked him in the arse a few times, you'd think he would remember how I fought. But did he? Pigs fly.

I waited till he was all but on me, then side-stepped neatly as a dancer, grabbed one of his lapels as he passed and turned him on my hip. Over he went into the dust, helped a little on his way by my boot in his crotch. I missed the main bits, actually, but caught him hard enough on the thigh to make him grunt and look afraid. I started to saunter away, pretending that it was all over, but knowing full well it was not. The crowd was growing festive and ugly and were throwing taunts. 'Queer boys' spat, eh?' shouted one man. Ranuccio picked up a stone and caught him clean between the eyes and he went down.

Curiously the crowd calmed a little after that.

Ranuccio came after me. And I kept my back to him, just slowed a little so I could hear his footsteps. And I slowed my breathing and relaxed until I could hear he was about just two steps from me and moving fast. I calculated he would just throw himself at me, which he duly did, so I bent my knees slightly and crumpled beneath him, so he went too high over my top, and then I straightened up and he flew high into the air sailing over my head and landing in the dust again. This time I gave him a good kicking for his troubles, including a beauty to his temple, which did not have my weight behind it, else he would be dead.

He lay awhile, shaking his head, and I gathered my breath. It wasn't over yet and I was beginning to enjoy myself. The crowd was too.

He was near a fountain at this point and paused to dunk his head and shoulders in, and he threw his head back and the spray around his head was all rainbow, rainbow.

The chants were growing uglier. I could hear the name of Fillide being bandied around and that was not good, for Ranuccio hated to be reminded of what a fool he was over that woman. He hated that worse than being called a butt-fucker. This could end badly. I went over and grabbed his hair and pulled his head back and put my mouth close to his ear. 'Go home,' I said as fierce as I could. 'Go home, for no good will come of this.'

And one in the crowd went, 'Ooooh, give him a kiss, then.' And fool that I was, I was distracted. Still, I punched the man's teeth in for it, which was something. Then I turned and Ranuccio was getting up, a bit groggily, but still with no intention of walking away.

He turned and drew and I could see how it would end. I knew that he was a better swordsman by far than I, but I also knew that I would kill him. And he knew it too. I have boxed, and wrestled and fenced, and I can tell you, I always know the outcome beforehand. Just look into the man's eyes. You will see victory or defeat there before a single blow is struck.

The boy threw me my sword, a perfectly judged throw, which I caught by lifting my hand in one brief movement, good boy, and Ranuccio brought his up and charged and we bickered around in the dust for a while, testing each other's blade for weak spots.

The cries from the onlookers were now deafening, and had taken a political turn. They were almost all on my side. 'Show the dirty Dago what for,' was the sort of thing I could hear ringing in my ears. 'Up the Spic's shit-chute,' was another. '*Vive la France*,' was another, although I never did see the logic of that one too much. Still, better to be ruled by the Frogs than the Dagos. Though better, far, by no one at all.

We were both on guard still, casually flicking our blades at each other, the high, bright tinkling of steel clearly audible over the shouts. He lunged, I parried, he lunged again, I parried and retreated a step. I felt curiously calm, and my rage was, as yet, not upon me. Just give me time, though. I felt just then a curious patience with this lad, as if I were a kindly uncle, indulging him in his tantrum. But God help him, if he does something to make me lose my patience. God help him. He knows what I am like. If he annoy me, let him look to his fate.

He got past one of my parries and nearly pinked my left side, but I fended it off with my left hand for his edge was angled inwards and I nudged only the flat. And so we carried on in the humid sweat of the afternoon, with Ranuccio slowly tiring as he lunged and lunged to increasingly little effect. I was content to play the long game. The crowd were getting a little bored and the taunts were becoming milder.

And then it all went to hell.

To my left, not far from the fountain, I saw the crowd murmur and part with a gentle rustle. And there, striding through the people, and now out into the open, came Giovan Tomassoni, who was Ranuccio's older brother and a good head and shoulders taller than him to boot, and about as wide as a stable door. Unlike Ranuccio, he was a battle-hardened soldier and had distinguished himself in the recent wars. The Spaniards had given him a medal, and everyone stood in awe of him. He had thrown his cloak aside and was carrying his heavy, unsheathed sword as he strode forward at a stately pace. And his brow was knitted so the eyebrows met in the middle and he had an air about him like the thunder that rumbled overhead. Oh, fuck.

And then there was a faint susurration in the crowd behind me, like a little stream when it runs over a shallow bank of pebbles. And I felt rather than saw a presence beside me. A brief flurry of a dropped cloak, that lovely, long, withdrawing zing as a sword is unsheathed, and God bless the very ground he treads on, it was little Minitti beside me. He is no soldier either, so to declare himself and stand up beside me at this hour was a truly brave thing. I reckoned the odds had now been reduced to about fifty to one against us.

And then another joined me. It was Troppa, a good man, but not one whom I had reckoned as a close friend before. You certainly discover who your friends are at times like this. And your enemies; another of Ranuccio's infernal brothers turfed up, almost as big as the first, and twice as ugly, and they all stood shoulder to shoulder sneering at us and swishing their blades in the dust. Ah, well. Time to get it done.

I let the two men on my wing choose their own men. I went for Ranuccio, and they all seemed happy to let me, because, as everyone knew, this was something personal. Now I was serious, though I would not show it yet.

But it was all over before it began. His temper was gone

and he was careless and doomed. There were a few moments, early on, when I thought I might spare him. But he was beginning to annoy me, and I was tired of my little games. Time to move on to something else. Some born fool came across the square and tried to put up our swords, so I swiped his heel and left him screaming and lame.

It was then that Ranuccio saw I was in earnest, so I feigned concern for the man I wounded and went to him. From the corner of my eye I saw Ranuccio coming and just before he struck I parried his blade, let it slide right up to my hilt, which has the horned catch upon it, and twisted. Not hard enough as it happened, for his blade did not snap, but hard enough for him to twist awkwardly and sprawl on the ground. And as he went down, I stamped hard with my heel on the side of his knee. There was a nasty crunching sound. Nothing was broken, I think, but some tendons had gone and he wasn't about to get up too quickly. He lay there, his mouth agape, clutching the side of his leg.

I stood up high and, quite slowly, lunged at his groin.

Not a killing thrust, you might think. Well, I had no mind to kill him just yet. I laughed out loud and told him he might soon know what it was like to sing castrato. In fact what I wanted to do was just nick him a little on the inner thigh, make him sting, but also frighten him.

And then disaster struck. The man I had wounded crawled up behind me and tugged at the back of my leg. My aim went awry, and before I could correct my stance, my blade entered Ranuccio's groin and stuck him like a hog. He did not cry out, which was strange, for the pain must have been terrible, but clutched himself and began to crawl away, lowing quietly like a heifer.

They carried him off quickly to a surgeon. Troppa, too, who looked in very bad shape, with slashes to his suit and blood all over his left arm and leg. And the others, Minitti and the two brothers, suddenly aghast, stopped almost in an instant and began to leave, first with a tiptoe, idle gait, then at a smarter pace, faster and faster until they were running. So too the crowd. The place was near deserted in a minute.

And as I walked away, I came in my breeches, but, strangely, my prick still stayed hard. And I felt an exaltation such as I have never known before. I must do that again.

The man who I had lamed rose from the ground without much sign of having been hurt and, hobbling only a little, threw a cloak above my shoulders, partially obscuring my face, and began to hustle me away. But I could see who he was now. It was Vialardi. And he certainly wasn't lame. Other hands belonging to the few remaining people arranged the cloak so that it covered more of my face, and urged me on and through the narrow streets, but it was Vialardi's hand that remained firm upon my elbow. My prick was still hard and I could feel my eyes were shining. But what in hell was Vialardi up to? I have often wondered, and never been entirely satisfied.

Is that it?

*Confiteor Deo omnipotenti . . . quia peccavi nimis cogitatione,
verbo et opere, mea culpa, mea culpa, mea maxima culpa.*

I confess to almighty God . . . that I have sinned exceedingly in
thought, word and deed, through my fault, through my fault, through
my most grievous fault.

The Ordinary of Mass. The Missal.

The Latin Eucharistic Liturgy used by the Roman Catholic Church
up to 1964

So there it is, I have told you of my major crime. Well, the
one that everyone knows about at any rate. As I said, the only
painting that I ever signed was a 'Beheading of John the
Baptist', and I wrote in the blood that flowed from his
severed neck *Feci Caravaggio*. I, Caravaggio, did this.

It is not much, is it? Not in the general scheme of things.
But there is more. Much more.

The Pope declared a death sentence upon me, and that is
why I fled Rome. It is a terrible thing to have hanging over
your head, for it may legally be carried out by anyone at any

time. So wherever you go, all men are your enemy, and you can look with open innocence on no one. A blow may come at any time, from a darkened doorway, from behind a screen in the inn bedchamber, from your fellow drinkers at the tavern. And you would never have time to make your peace with the world.

I like that. It is finally my natural state. Let me carry my rage to the next place beyond the grave, wherever it be. I will burn, I know it, but better that, than serve.

Malta

The dawn of a summer day in July.

Lead.

Slate.

Then onion.

Pearl.

And all about me the quiet lapping of water. I said before that I hated boats, and so I do, but this crossing was a quiet one and seemed to me auspicious. I had hated Naples, where I had fled. True, it was outside the juris-diction of the Pope, but still it was on a mainland which was buzzing with my story, and you never knew where a blow might come from. The Pope had put *bando capitale* on my head.

That's not just any old death sentence. Oh no, it means that anyone, anywhere, at any time can grab you and take you back to Rome, where, in the due course of Papal Law in all its awful majesty, you are denied any trial whatsoever and summarily executed by axe, garrote or fire according to your station in life.

There is a simpler alternative for any righteous, law-abiding, fine, upstanding man who can't be bothered to undertake the tiresome business of holding me prisoner all the way back to Rome. Simply strike me dead where I stand, lop off my head, take it back to Rome and you can lawfully claim your due reward.

So I could not lay my head to rest of an evening without wondering whether it would be my last. What villain was lurking behind the curtains? What bounty-man waiting outside the tavern? Who knows where the killing blade might come from? Think about living like that. It can make a man edgy.

I spent perhaps a year in Naples, dashing out canvases at a rate of knots. I have always worked fast, for no better reason than simply because that is the way I happen to work. But now I had good reason to do so. I feel time's wings beating at my back. I need money and I need it now. And my life is suddenly bounded, bracketed, confined by the edict of the Holy One. If I am going to be killed tomorrow at least I will have them say that I was cut down in my prime. It's the only revenge I can think of at the moment.

Think? I can barely talk, let alone gather two consecutive thoughts together. I walk like a sleeper. I hardly notice where I am going sometimes. But it has sharpened my other senses. I can hear a man in his stockings walking around a corner from a mile away. And I can smell him before he has entered my room. I can smell whether he has been eating meat or fish or only vegetables before he is over the threshold. This is not idle boast. I could always smell a man when his temper was up. Now I am even more acute.

My sight was always good. But colour now takes on even greater riches. I no longer need the bright blues and reds, which I did so delight in when I was young. I see a hundred times more beauty now in a dark brown, or the pale tints of quiet flesh. Or a ray of light across a fur or a beaten earth floor or a suit of black armour. Such colours do not distract the eye, but rather let it concentrate on my forte, the human face. There I will have my theatre, there my drama, there my applause.

So I tired of my Spanish masters in Naples, and all the praise they heaped upon me. Suddenly fame was not such a great thing to have hanging around one's neck. It aroused not just the usual envy among others, but murderous instincts too.

I bought a passage, at the last minute, on one of the galleys to Malta. And now I watch dawn break over the horizon of the ocean Terrene and the coal-black sea. The galley slaves, short-term criminals in the main, have been straining since before dawn. Poor bastards. I have done any number of things that could have put me in their place. But blind luck, or patronage, have kept me out of prison and galley alike. Until now however. My luck ran out with that Ranuccio. And his too, now I think of it.

Malta was like a brand-new city in miniature. All the buildings in the centre were fresh built and well looked after. And the streets were all laid out in a regular square pattern, as if someone had planned the whole place from scratch only a few years before and torn down all the poor houses. Which they tell me is roughly what happened. The Knights of the Order of St John who run the place have a long, fierce history of which they are very proud. In fact they are proud of everything about themselves, and on balance I think they have every right to be.

They are descended, although they deny it fiercely, from the Knights Templars, who used to keep the Holy Land safe for pilgrims, but who grew so rich and powerful that the greedy King of France cast envious eyes on them and had them all burnt at the stake, accusing them of witchcraft and sodomy and being Cathar heretics and God knows what else, just any bloody thing that would give him a good excuse to wipe them out entirely and take their money. Which he duly did, or at least he thought he did. But the wily Templars lived on in secret, some say in Scotland, some say in under ground cells scattered through southern France, some say in those secret societies called Masons.

Originally garrisoned on Rhodes, which they lost to the Turks, the knights then came to Malta not so long ago as a bulwark against the Turk pirates who rape the seas hereabouts. And about fifty years ago, before I was born, they thrashed the Turks in a huge sea battle with terrible losses to both sides. This was before Lepanto, though they took an honourable part in that too. Valetta was besieged by the Turk fleet and it is said that they took their Christian prisoners and crucified them all, and pushed the still living bodies out into the sea so that the knights awoke to find the piteous cries of their dying friends floating in the harbour. There is nothing your Muslim won't do.

Still, the knights got their retaliation in very nicely. They beheaded all their Turkish prisoners, packed their cannon with the heads, and fired them all over into the Turkish fleet. That enraged the Turks, you can bet. And living proof that whatever else people say about the Knights of Malta, they still have a good sense of humour.

They are a pretty austere bunch these days, living here in this arid, waterless place. There are no rivers on Malta, nor streams, and water has to come from wells. No trees neither. It's a hot island, and a dull one. Not much happens and people spend a large part of the day snoozing. They have dedicated their lives to Christ but also to fighting, which strikes me as a strange combination, but never mind, because I like fighting as much as the next man. Especially if the next man happens to be a Jesuit secret agent.

And they have great prestige. From all over Europe, young men travel here in the hope, sometimes vain, of being accepted into the garrison. They must be of aristocratic lineage, well enough off, and keen. It takes at least a year of praying, fasting and weapon instruction, as well as a sound knowledge of the order's history, before they qualify to be a knight. Quite a tall order for any man, and many are refused, though there be no shame in that.

To have a title and bear arms and wear a tabard with the white silk Maltese cross would be very wonderful. A man I once challenged, years ago in my travels outside Rome, looked down his nose at me from his horse and said that since he was a knight and I was a commoner, he could not take up the challenge since it was beneath him. I was so shocked that I did not attack, and went away and seethed with indignation and humiliation for days.

I want to be a knight.

Maybe the Pope will give me my pardon quicker if I am made a knight. But who cares if he doesn't, I'd still be Sir Michelangelo Merisi da Caravaggio. It has a ring to it, don't you think?

The Colonna family, who own the galleys and had been looking after my welfare for so long now, organized a travelling companion for me, a kindly fellow and a knight too. He talked to me almost continually during the voyage about the knights and how they lived and their history, which I have just passed on to you. For he realized just by being with me that I suffered terribly with *mal de mer*, and he did indeed succeed in keeping me distracted so that it was much easier than usual. He was so kind, but without undue ostentation, so that you scarce noted the kindness being done, which I take to be a very knightly virtue. And when we disembarked he took me to the apothecary and gave me herbs which settled my stomach and my shaky legs almost immediately and then found me lodgings within the barracks, and within a day or two introduced me to Alof de Wignacourt, who is the head man around here.

And to Malaspina, who was my passport to the island and to any future success I might have. Malaspina was related in some distant way that I can't be bothered to go into (wife's uncle or some such) to my last patron in Naples. Word had reached him of my art and he was anxious to get a painting out of me for his chapel in the main cathedral on Malta. The cathedral serves the Knights of Malta, and since they are divided into seven different chapters or *langues*, each one staffed by knights of the same nationality, there are separate chapels for each nationality. Malaspina's chapel was for the Italians, and so he wanted a St Jerome, a man I done often enough before. I had always varied the composition and features of the saint to suit the patron, and now was no different.

Jerome you will recall is the old man in a big round red cardinal's hat, who is always in his study, surrounded by dusty old books, busy writing the Bible at his desk, or rather translating it. For some reason which I have never discovered he is usually portrayed as having a pet lion, although in all the old paintings I have seen, the lion looks more like a pussycat with big teeth. This is probably because none of the painters had seen a lion. Well, I haven't seen a lion either, which is exactly the reason why I am not going to put one in the painting. If someone can show me a lion, then I might paint one, but not until. You know my rules well enough by now. Only from life, only from life.

So I did Jerome, but I was a little bit cunning. I had been introduced to Alof de Wignacourt, the head knight, and had watched him around the place, bearing himself with great dignity and striking inspiring poses and generally ordering people around. He was every inch the soldier, with an erect bearing and fine, fit body even though he must have been at least sixty.

So I gave Jerome just a hint of Alof's features. And painted him as if he were a military commander, aroused from his camp bed in his tent and writing orders. His body is old and gaunt, but still well-muscled and rangy. His head is bald and there is grey in his beard, but the jaw is still firm and the eyes and brow show a fixity of purpose. My Jerome is a very active Jerome. And it was designed to stand along a doorway, so I did a fake door edge down the left-hand side of the frame and put the Malaspina coat of arms on it. Also a very nice skull on the desk as a reminder of the grim reaper, and a crucifix in fake perspective, also on the desk projecting out at the viewer. All in all, I like this one. He's my kind of Jerome, a warrior saint.

Alof liked it too. I said I used a bit of cunning, but it

doesn't take much, for men are so vain. I never met one who didn't want his portrait done, and while it was being done, would say, 'Now, I am not a vain man, but . . .' and then they would say that they were not quite so bald six months ago, so could you put a bit more hair in, or, my eyesight is only bad of late, so could I not squint so much as I do, or, please paint my right profile, for the wart on the left of my nose is unbecoming to a man of my status.

So it was with Alof. The wart, I mean. He had a real beauty, nestling in the valley where his left nostril joined his face. Christ it was hard talking to him, you could hardly tear your eyes away from that thing. It practically glowed in the dark like a lighthouse. And conversation was hard too. You only had to mention some subject like the weather and you'd be saying how wart it was for the time of year; or ships, and you'd be talking about how something was athwart the vessel. Never mind.

He just loved my Jerome, and I don't think he even saw through my little plan. He just looked at the saint and declared it a masterpiece without ever thinking once that he was almost looking in a mirror. Nor did he mention my military conceit. To him it was just some clerk, working late into the night on his Bible. 'Damn scribblers, they ought to get out and about a bit more in the sunshine. See the world. Learn some discipline. Never did me any harm.' You know the kind of man, I am sure. A bore in peacetime, but when the Turk comes calling he's the man you want up on your wall.

Anyway he decided to commission me to do his portrait, which would hang up in the main dining room, along with all his dead predecessors, including the fabled Jean de la Valette, who defeated the Turkish fleet that I told you about, and after whom I believe Valetta is now called. His portrait did him no justice, incidentally.

I devised a plan for Alof, since he was a busy man and couldn't sit still for more than two minutes at a stretch without barking out an order at a pageboy to go and see to something in the garrison. I put him in armour.

That would keep him still, I thought. Not a bit of it, though. The cunning old bastard just propped up the front bits of his armour, the cuirass and shin guards and so on, and left the back off, so he could just step in and out of the things at will. Still, it didn't finally matter. I trapped him on a Sunday, in between prayers, when he didn't have much to do, and got all his face done in one go. And then concentrated on his armour at my leisure.

And what a face it was. Leonine, grizzled, a face that could stare down the sun. His hair was receding, but he had a magnificent spade-cut beard, which jutted forward into your face. He stood four-square and had that air of command about him that comes to men of his calling and stature. He could give you an order and you would follow him anywhere. He had a good humour too, and I showed that.

The armour was a bit of a problem. I spent too long on the delicate filigree engravings on it. I could hardly do otherwise, since most painters would use an assistant to fill in this sort of thing, but I never use one, as you know. And it needed doing, and in a way it was a good technical challenge, to catch all that gold and bronze and silver with just base colours. But eventually I got bored with it, and didn't bother to correct its stance, which is crude and mechanical and does not appear to be fitted to a man inside it. The light glinting off the black arms and legs is good, for I had already done something similar in *The Taking of Christ*. But the arms are stiff. He is holding a mace of office in his left hand and slapping the palm of his right hand with it. It is awkward, I know it, but then he was a left hander. And he is wearing gauntlets too.

I haven't mentioned the pageboy. And I hardly know where to start, for he got me into so much trouble. And out of it too, some time later.

There were many pageboys on the island, each knight claiming to require at least one for their wardrobe and especially for the care of their arms and armour. Indeed, under Alof, they had increased three- or fourfold in number. I will say no more than that; although there was much speculation and whispering in dark corners as to why.

A Long Digression on the Order

A new kind of monster, compounded of purity
and corruption, a monk and a knight.

Henry of Huntingdon (1084-1155) *Historia Anglicorum*.
Of Henry of Blois (1101-71), Bishop of Winchester and brother of King Stephen.

A word here, perhaps, about the knights is in order. I did much reading in the fortress library, with a little help from Malaspina, for my Latin letters are not what they might be. He also showed me around the fortress's museum, which contains many relics of the knights' great deeds. It seems that the original order of the Knights Templar was disbanded under grave circumstance. They had, as I said, originated during the Crusades, and set up and maintained castles for the safety of visiting pilgrims. They looked after the sick like the Hospitallers. But as the years went by they became bankers and so very wealthy.

If a pious merchant wanted to visit the shrine of the Sepulchre, well good for him, the knights would help all they could. The journey could take anything up to a year from London or the Baltic states, the seas were hazardous and the land routes crawling with bandits. So the good gentleman was a bit worried about carrying too much money with him. No problem, said the knights. Just lodge a nice fat casket of your wife's jewellery with us, we give you a letter of credit you can keep safe tucked up inside your corsets, and then when you reach Jerusalem, you can cash it in at our special agency we have set up for that very purpose.

So the knights realized something that most ordinary men do not. You will never get wealthy by working for someone else. And it is easier and better paid to set up a bank than to rob one. And they became very, very wealthy indeed.

As for the pilgrims who did finally make it, and knelt at the Holy Stone and then came back, well, good for them, that should earn a few extra years at the right hand of God. But they had still left a tidy sum with the good knights and of course it all earned interest at the usual Jew rates, and that soon adds up when a man is away for at least a year on a pilgrimage.

Some said that they indulged in alchemy too, and I can well believe that they did. Of course, for the swine of the Inquisition this was tantamount to witchcraft, but then anything is tantamount to witchcraft if it suits their purpose. My friend Bruno was often trying out alchemical pursuits and they often succeeded. He said that the idea was, in fact, not to create gold, but to change base earthly matter into something spiritual and other-worldly.

I forget how he worked it exactly, but anyway, he did quite often cause a huge explosion among his flasks and tubes, and we'd all rush in and there he would be, standing there with his clothes smouldering and no eyebrows, and there'd be a little puddle of gold on the dish in front of him, still molten from the blast. And he'd mutter and curse and throw it in the fire, saying that wasn't what he wanted at all, blasted modern gold-diggers, they had ruined the whole thing, not like it was in my day, all purity and search for knowledge and so on. And he would 'Harumph', and 'Bah' and stagger out, pulling on his beard and showering dandruff everywhere and start planning his next explosion almost straight away, but with a new formula this time, one with less potash maybe.

Poor Bruno, I did love him so and there is never a day goes by that I do not call him to mind and wish him a better afterlife than he found here on earth. He was a good man and I do believe he will find it. And never can I forgive the Jesuits for burning him. I have said that often enough in the past, but I will keep repeating it, lest I get soft and think perhaps that they had their reasons too.

I am hell-bound, I know it, but I will see them there with me, I know that. Else there is no justice.

Sorry, where was I . . .? Yes, so they were bankers and they had the secret of making gold. What else? Well, they set up their own courier service too, adopting the name of the Thurn and Taxis family, the best the world has ever seen, but I will tell you about that later when I come to it. For it has some bearing on my story. Please be patient and abide with me.

The King of France had grown greedy for their wealth, and the Pope was jealous of their power, and so between them they got up charges of heresy, rounded them all up from their castles in southern France or Provence, put them to the rack and burned the lot of them, every man jack including their fabled leader Jacques de Molay, a great man by all accounts. Apparently they all went uncomplaining to their deaths, which I find hard to account for, except that, as was explained to me, they had made provision for the Order to continue in secret. Some say they formed the Free-masons, others that they became followers of the Rosy Cross (*Ros* being the alchemical term for dew, an important element in certain explosions), others yet that they slowly transmuted into the current order of the Knights of St John in Malta. Whatever the truth, there were ugly charges brought against them during the trials, with witchcraft and alchemy and such being bandied about. Sodomy being the main one.

They always throw that one in, it's a guarantee of success. It seems that this was the main charge bought against them by the courts of the Inquisition. Some had been known anyway as the Bougres, from the roots of some of the knights in Bulgaria, and everyone knows what the Bulgarians get up to on their nights off.

So, here you have all these hairy, sweaty warriors, all with their blood up from having bashed up the wicked infidel Arab and galloping around the desert at top speed, cutting off heads. And what do they do when they burst through the gates of the city they were besieging? Well, what do any soldiers do? They indulge themselves in the classic spoils of war; knock back a quick bottle of the local wine, and then it's downtown for a bit of looting here and a bit of raping there.

But here is the catch. The poor bastards have taken a vow of chastity. So there they are, panting and heaving in the town square that they have just captured by storming through a breach in the wall at much expense of blood and battered bones. And there are the brutish footsoldiers, all going at the local women like steam hammers, and the local women protesting a bit just for form's sake, and then indulging themselves in a bit of well-earned fun.

And what do the knights do? I will tell you what they are supposed to do. Erm . . . look up to heaven, try to think of something other than bashing the bishop, ask for forgiveness, go back to the garrison by way of the chapel first, then not wash off the dust and sweat from their bodies as a penance, thirty quick lashes with their own scourge to further distract their minds, and retire to bed to think pure thoughts all alone all night long. That is what is written in the rulebook.

Eh?

Pardon me if I doubt it somehow. Men are men, no matter what their best intentions. Short of hacking it off, you can't keep a young man's dick down, it has a mind of its own. So what did they do of a night once they were back in their garrison? Well, you tell me.

Then there were other accusations. That the knight's initiation into the order involved spitting on the Cross. And renouncing the true Christ. And worshiping a demon called Baphomet in the shape of cat. And kissing the chief knight upon the arse, in a demonic perversion of the ritual of kissing the Pope's ring.

All true, said Jacques de Molay before they burned him. A very odd admission, I find that. Why would a good stout-hearted man, who had dedicated his life to doing the right thing, admit to such foulness? Well, he sort of mumbled some explanation apparently. The knights were being trained for what might happen to them if they were captured by the Muslim. They would be required to spit on the cross and renounce their calling to Christ. Best get them used to the idea beforehand, said Molay. Anyway, it was only pretend, they could spit on the ground near the cross and not onto the thing itself.

And the kissing of the arse of a fellow knight? Um, well, another ritual to get you used to such foulness, because who knows what the Arab will inflict upon you, what with their women being veiled and kept indoors all the time, they are all walking around thinking of nothing else and just bound to jump on some poor Christian prisoner and give him a good length up the windward passage. Best be prepared, boys, so get your best pal to spread 'em.

And Baphomet? Oh, there were cats around all over the place, useful as mousers, don't you know? And some of them did look a bit sinister, the Egyptians used to worship them too. I dare say some knight or other got one dragged up to look like a demon one night, schoolboy prank, high spirits, that sort of thing.

And on the charge of sodomy?

No one said a word.

It was literally the 'unspeakable' crime. You had best not even mention it at all. For it was the gravest offence, and all heaven cried out against it for vengeance. And you would surely burn for it if discovered. But if another man accused you of it, and the accusation was found false, then he himself would burn for such a vile calumny.

Hardly surprising that it wasn't much talked about, is it?

Still, they burned the lot of them. Except that there is one enduring part of the tale. Every account of the whole horrid purging tells that the local authorities, bailiffs, sheriffs and so on were very unhappy about the King's orders to round up all the knights. After all, they were locals and neighbours and not a bad lot at all, since they looked after you when you were ill and generally kept the local *banditi* in their place. And so they sent around various officials to survey all the knights' lodgings and goods and chattels, some two days before they were due to be rounded up. It was a pretty obvious warning. In fact, it was all but a nudge in the ribs and a huge wink and a tap on the side of the nose. But did the knights take the hint? No, they did not.

But, and here all the accounts agree too, a huge haystack was seen leaving the main castle on a cart, just two days before the authorities descended on the knights. And was never seen again.

Who knows what it contained? There have been endless rumours. The Holy Grail, perhaps, for the finding of the Grail was one of the knights' earliest pursuits? Several of the most learned knights, perhaps, the ones most steeped in their esoteric lore? Or heaps of their treasure? Or some of the more lusty young ones, under orders to breed and continue the order elsewhere? Some even say that what they called Baphomet was in fact the most desirable relic of all, the relic to beat all relics: the Head of Christ. And it was hidden in the hay. Just think of it, Jesus's Head! Now that would be something, wouldn't it? Better than all those dirty bits of rag and bone which the priests are always telling us are His robes or a little-known saint's finger.

Who knows, it may all be true, or none of it. History is only the lies that the present tells us in order to summon the past.

The Pageboy

The round universe is the plaything of a boy

Walter Bagehot. *National Review. 1856*

That's enough history, where was I? Oh yes, Alof and his pageboy.

I am sure you catch my drift. A little sodomy was not completely unknown in this celibate sect of warriors.

Anyway, I did this portrait of Alof and he was mighty pleased with it, went around puffed up like a pigeon for days, sticking his chest out and ruffling his feathers. Pathetic, really, it's always so easy to please people. I painted his face in right-hand profile (to hide the wart), and made him look almost human, which he often did not.

And I put in his pageboy. I didn't mention that, did I? Well, I didn't like to, for he is an angelic, golden-haired lad of maybe fourteen summers. And he is gorgeous.

Now before you get all prim and start accusing me of betraying my sexual tastes (as if I care, now), let me say that there is an admirable precedent in the works of the one man I will admit to being a master. Tiziano of Venice, whom men call Titian, did a similar thing once with a marchese, I forget his name, addressing his troops. It's in the Prado now, but never mind that, it was in Venice when I was there. And the marchese is up on his podium holding forth with a very camp declamatory gesture such as actors use in tragedy, shouting away fit to bust at his warriors, waving his arm around, exhorting them to ever greater feats of butchery. And just on his right, snug in the corner of the frame, is his pageboy, looking coyly out at the viewer and pouting slightly. Well, guess where your eye goes?

So I did something similar with Alof's portrait. The boy is nicely clad in dark velvet doublet and red stockings and neat little lace collar and cuffs. He is holding up Alof's great helmet, with white and red plumes, to the maestro, though not so much offering it to him as showing the thing off a bit. I did a bit of mischief with his legs. From the waist up, it is clear that he is standing slightly ahead of his master, the helmet partly obscures the knight's elbow. But below the waist, the page's feet are in line with the knight, so that he should be standing beside him. Let future art lovers puzzle over that. They'll say I didn't finish it, or that an inept pupil finished it for me, or I was in a hurry and made a hash of it. I couldn't care less, it just amuses me.

I had done something similar once, when I had left off St Francis's legs altogether, he was just lying asleep in his habit and there was nothing showing below the waist. No one noticed. I sometimes wonder why I bother painting at all.

No, I don't. It is the one thing that keeps me from going mad in this world. And I don't always enjoy it, but I do enjoy getting it done. Starting is always hell, but wiping my brushes at the end, and putting them away, always pleases me, and to get to that point, one has to have started.

The page has inclined his head, as if peeking around the edge of the frame having just spotted his audience and putting on a sweet smile of welcome. His blonde hair is close cropped and he has large dark eyes.

Jesus Maria, I could happily go to prison for him.

Which is precisely what I did.

I will tell you about it later, for it ended my stay on the island, but there is some matter worth telling beforehand, and I will keep things in order so far as I can with my faltering memory.

A Missive

To:

His Beatitude Pope Paul V.

From:

Alof de Wignacourt, head of the Knights of Malta, Valetta, Malta.

Delivered through the office of Marcellus, Maltese Ambassador to the Holy See

MOST SECRET

Accept this only from the hand of Sir Alonso de Contreras, special courier in the service of the Thurn and Taxis Postal Company for the Knights of Malta. If the seal be broken, or tampered with, imprison the courier, burn the missive, inform the sender and await further instructions.

Your Holiness,

The Order of the Knights of Malta now have the opportunity of acquiring to the service of our religion a most virtuous person of the most honoured qualities and whom we hold our particular servant. May I take this occasion to humbly remind you that the Order of St John has always had the right to confer upon a chosen candidate the right to a knighthood, while dispensing with the normal probationary period. In order that we do not lose the services of this most valued person, newly arrived on this island, I must ask you, through my ambassador, to kindly allow the Order once only to confer the magistral habit on this person without obligation of trial, and that having committed homicide in a brawl should not be an obstacle to him, for many of our knights have so transgressed, and it is not always an obstacle to a good knight.

When and if he is granted the dispensation, the candidate would straight away share the other knights' rights of canteen and allowance. The matter is most intensely desired by us, so we most warmly urge the matter upon you and await its earliest possible resolution. We shall pay all costs involved.

Reply

To:

Alof de Wignacourt, in Valetta, Malta.

From:

His Holiness, The Pope in Rome.

Via the office of: Marcellus, Maltese Ambassador to Rome

Accept only from the hand of Fra Anthony, of the Vatican Courier Service.

Conditions as previously.

Not secret.

As to your prospective knight, even though he has committed homicide in a brawl, as long as there is not other legal impediment, then let your wish be mine also. And much good may it do him.

A Spring

So there it is. They brought me the news early one morning and by the next day it was done. No scrabbling around in the mud for me. No lining up for the tourney, no jousting practice, no silly initiation rites from the other knights, just up one morning and they put the chain round my neck and a tabard with the Maltese Cross on it, and a big and solemn service in the cathedral, and suddenly everyone is bowing and scraping and calling me 'sir'. I love it. At last I feel as though I belong.

I stepped out from my room that day with a spring in my step such as I had not felt since the brawl in Rome and my flight. The sun was back in the sky, and perhaps one day soon the Pope would lift the sentence, as he surely must for a knight. But still, this cursed itch is upon me, and I cannot do anything to scratch it unless . . . I must paint. You'd think that a knight would suddenly be free of such drives, wouldn't you? Alas, no, it made me feel a lot better about things in general, but still I have this urge that is far, far worse than addiction to drug or strong drink. I am not satisfied until I am drying off my brushes for the last time, and then it lasts anything up to a month before it strikes again. No amount of drinking or whoring can make it go away. And God knows I have tried hard enough in both those lines. Not even killing a man will do it, and I've tried that.

Time to give something back to the Order, I thought. And the thought came to me even at the induction ceremony in the cathedral. I looked around the oratory. It was a large empty place, and there above the altar was just the place for a big wide canvas. I did not even have to rack my brains for a subject. St John has always been one of my favourite saints, whether idling in the wilderness or having his head cut off for some dancing tart. And of course he is the patron saint of the knights. What else then could I do? When the obvious is presented before us as the only choice, then the dreadful uncertainties of freedom are removed. All we can do is what we must.

I chose to do a beheading. Must I go into why for you? Thank you, I thought not.

I may have no taste to put architecture in my paintings, but I can do it well enough as you may know. I think I told you that buildings were among the first things I drew, perhaps because my father was sometime an architect of a small sort. Also because buildings stand still, which for a six-year-old is quite important. I often think that I learnt to frighten people at an early age simply so I could get them to stand still. So I can paint a building with the best of them. If I choose not, it is for a number of reasons. Mainly, because I want only to paint the human face and form. But I also have at the back of my mind the awful hash I got into over my first big commissioned painting, *The Martyrdom of St Matthew*, where I paid too much heed to the patron's written instructions on the subject, even though he was already dead, for Heaven's sake. I will never forget the sweat and the hot flushes that gave me when I realized that I was slowly painting myself further and further up a dead end. It was only turning to some other painting that I managed to turn my mind around and escape. To this day it haunts me, and never will I renounce my vow of painting exactly how and what I want and nothing else.

So. I used a small courtyard that I had seen on Valetta, it was not very far from the cathedral and even a novice knight, contemplating my painting in the oratory, might well stumble out into the daylight and find himself, quite soon, exactly in the spot of my beheading. Woof, that might bring him up short. I tell you this now as more or less an after-thought, I do not think it was foremost in my mind at the time of painting, though perhaps it was at the back of my thoughts. It would have a good effect upon a novice, to think upon his patron saint.

And also on the manner of his death, for many, many knights have been martyred in the cause of their vocation by this very means. The Turk cut off their heads in their hundreds. So just as the skull in my Jerome is my memento mori, so too is this whole composition of John being beheaded a little reminder to the initiates of what might be awaiting them. A grisly thought, which makes me smile inside a little. Or it did, until I remembered that I still had the Pope's sentence hanging on my head. That rather took the edge off my knighthood, I can tell you. I don't know if the Pope knows that it was me that Alof got a special dispensation for. I suspect not. Oh, shit, still running for my life.

The courtyard was simple enough, all in shades of brown, a simple archway, a simple barred window off to the right through which two prisoners watch. That isn't in the courtyard, but I know prisons well enough. And I know that view through bars. There are times when I feel I am in one here on the island, it is so small, and I am indentured to the Order as surely as any slave. But never mind, I must not complain. The saint is already dead, I had decided on that at an early stage and painted him first, so the model could go after less than a day, before I got down to the hard stuff. I could have done the prisoners first too, but wanted to test their facial reactions. So I got the thug in and had him pose, hunched over the ground, reaching for his knife at his waistband in order to finish the bloody deed of cutting off John's head. It was a pose I recall seeing somewhere else, in a Perseus I think it was, in Venice, I forget who the painter was, but I recall the pose only too well. But it was all no good.

I needed John back. I needed to see the thug's expression as he prepared to cut a dead man's head off. And I needed to see the reactions of the onlookers. You know me by now. Only from life, only from life.

It wasn't hard on my John. He just had to lie there. But it was hard on the executioner to start with. He was bent double at the waist and then twisted through a half turn too, with his arm arched back uncomfortable. Still I had his outline done with the butt end of my brush in only a couple of minutes. And then I had done the bulk of him in less than an hour. And the highlights could come later. And by the end of that hour, as the sweat dripped down his face to the end of his nose in the sultry heat of an August afternoon, his face had assumed a mask of utter indifference, with just a wrinkled brow, as if this were just the last task to be performed at the end of another long day of boring work. And I was about to shout at him, when I realized that this was perfect and just what I wanted. He may have been an executioner, but as far as he was concerned, his was a job of work just like any other. Another head to be lopped off by hand? All in a day's work, squire. Where do you want it?

Perfect. There is a limit to the amount that a man can be horrified. After a while, he is inured to the worst. You will find it in soldiers. And doctors too. And me.

Salome is my Fillide as best I can remember her. God I wish she were here, dark-eyed houri that she was. She comes to me still in my dreams, and troubles me there. And when I smell sandalwood, it is as if she is there next to me, naked in the same room. Just that smell can give me a hard-on. Perhaps one day artists will find a way of reproducing smell, as an aide-memoire. For smell is the most evocative of our senses.

The pointing jailer is in the costume of the Turk. Just a reminder to my brother knights.

I used only browns and blacks, as is my habit these days, but in a flurry of eagerness I gave John a bright red sash. He was dead after all, and he deserved a little luxury. Besides it took me back a little to my early days, when I was just beginning to paint for money and the world looked like a new place, because I did not fully comprehend it. Now I do, and believe me it looks shabby.

And in the blood that flows from his neck, I did something I had never done before. It came to me suddenly, in an access of joy such as I had not felt since a child.

I signed the painting. Not just with my name, but something more. Read it closely and you will find: *F Michel A*.

You may take that F as standing for Fra, or Brother in Knighthood.

Or you may take it as something else altogether; *Feci Michel A.*

I, Michelangelo da Caravaggio, did this.

The old lady on the left, though, she is something else. Note that she is covering not her eyes, but her ears. Perhaps she cannot bear to hear the truth.

And the face of the executioner? That, you will surely know. Look at the portraits of myself done by Minitti. Or look at my use of Ranuccio as an assassin. Look in the mirror if you must. Think of whosoever you wish. You may see my hand anywhere and all about.

It was my best painting to date, I think. And believe me I do not always believe my latest to be my best. I am variable, I know it, and I dot backward and forward in my subjects, in my scale and in my style. I do not always progress. But here I have. I do believe I have reached my current limit. Perhaps, like Alexander at the edge of the known world, I will sit down on the shore and weep for having no more left to conquer.

And the strange thing is that I have not done anything new in the picture. I have used old faces, as best as I could remember them. I have used old poses, some from paintings I saw about me in Venice and other places, some from my own previous inventions. I have used old lighting; my usual single light source, slanting diagonal-wise across the whole scene, a bit like you will find sometimes in theatres. And I have used old colours, my ochres and umbers and all shades of brown, aside from that brief flurry of red.

And above all I did it fast. I have told you that I always work at a lick. It is the only way for the painting to keep up with my thoughts. If I have a new thought or idea, then I must get it down on canvas fast, for it soon evaporates and is replaced by something newer. It is that way with me and writing. That is why I do not write. I find the process so slow and cumbersome that I have finished a letter or story in my head long before I can set it all down. And so I get bored and am not true to myself.

Here I worked almost at the speed of thought. I did not even have time to fill in all the mass areas of paint. So the brush strokes were swift and sometimes I let the canvas or ground colour show through the stroke and, rather than go back and fill in, I let it stand. The effect pleased me. It is all less realistic than I sometimes do, and tends towards more of an impression of the scene, as might be seen at a quick glance or through a brief window. It is better to stand back from it than close in, which again is good, for it will stand some distance off behind an altar. I said it was less realistic, but when looked at right, it is more so. I know not how to explain it, for I think at last that with this picture I have exceeded my intentions. You must look for yourself.

There it is for all time. I, Caravaggio, did this. You may read my signature how you will. I once butchered a man in hot blood with my sword, and Ranuccio was not the only one either. And I too have a price on my own head, just as did St John. And I did this painting, which I think my summit. Judge me on all counts if you wish. Or any of them singly on their merits. Damn me for ever for my sins. Or burn all my canvases until none remain for whatever iniquity you think I have visited upon the craft of picture making. But remember this at all time and on any or all of the counts or whatever punishment you devise for me. I do not care what you think.

So I finished and I took my small brush, the last one I had used, the one with the fine point, to put on my signature and I took the rag in my left hand and I placed the hairs of the brush on the rag, with a little oil, and I clasped the hairs with my fingers around the tip and pulled the brush out through the rag. And I lingered a little on the process, arching my back for it ached, and twisting my head, for I had a crick in my neck. And those aches were delicious, the true signs of a hard job done. And the wiping of the brush, I do not always like to think too heavily on that, in case the pleasure should one day desert me. But it never has so far. And I cannot cheat. I wipe my brushes at the end of each day, when it is time to pause over a painting, but I never gain any pleasure in doing so. Not until I have put the final strokes to the picture, then and only then is there justice and finality and pleasure in the wiping of a brush.

A friend of mine who is a poet, a good one too for patrons pay him good money for his occasional verse, once said to me that a poem is never finished only abandoned, and that he is always tempted to return to it and improve it. He said that he expected I felt the same about my paintings.

I do not. I know exactly when my picture is ended. And I have often finished with it before it looks finished. Hence funny little problems like that one with the pageboy's legs in Alof's portrait. I was done with the picture before I put them in, so I just couldn't be bothered to do it properly. Are you with me? I suspect those of you who understand have a finer understanding of my art than those who think me lazy or stupid. But think what you like. Think me stupid if you like. I told you before, I do not care for your opinion or indeed for any other's. I have been paid well enough for my pictures by men who could not read them. No doubt I will be looked at in the future by other men equally ignorant. That idea used to enrage Baglione, the stupid little turd. Me, it just makes me laugh. I believe it is called irony.

So they took it and hung it up and Alof was so pleased with it that he gave me a gold chain and two slaves. The gold chain I sold and spent the money by gambling on a race and then bought an evening with three whores. They played naked leapfrog for me and that was a sight. Never seen that one before. These Maltese are beginning to impress me as an inventive race. They like pornography too, so I did a little sideline in that, drawing the whores in all sorts of interesting positions and sold them down at the harbour to the sailors. Poor bastards, they can't get a woman from one month to the next, and so it's five-fingered Mary and her horny-palmed sister in their hammock each night.

The two slaves I set free and then fucked. They couldn't believe their luck. They thought I would fuck them while they were still slaves. Getting it the other way around made them so grateful.

So all was going swimmingly now, what with me a knight, something I never, ever thought I would get this side of heaven, and Alof chortling with glee every time he looks on me and beams like a father with a new babe. He must have taken quite a risk asking the Pope to allow a knighthood on me, although I would like to bet that he did not actually mention me by name, but rather hinted about some painter or other. I can just see the Pope giving birth there and then, giving birth to triplets at the thought of giving Caravaggio a knighthood.

And Alof thinks he has pulled it all off, what with me being the greatest painter in all Christendom, and him having a handsome new portrait to show off to *hoi polloi*. Poor silly bastard. He should have known me better, for if he had, he never would have come within shouting distance of me. He should have sent an armed guard to Valetta harbour and forcibly turned my boat around and told me to fuck off out of his island and go to hell, where I belonged, and never darken his palace step again. Because it wasn't long before it all turned to shit for me. It always does.

On the subject of new-born babes, I did a little one for a man I met on the island, a steward like my father, whose wife had just given birth. I owed him some drink money, so I paid with a painting as I often do. People seem to like it that way. It was only a little thing, a child asleep, but I dressed it up like a Cupid, with wings behind it and a broken bow and arrow. The whole looks a bit sombre, for my backgrounds are becoming more and more dark (you may guess why), but there is affection there, which I took from the father's face, even though he is not in the painting, and let it shine through. The baby is quite ugly, but parents always do feel kindly toward such a vulnerable thing, especially when asleep. He was most pleased.

And that was the last picture I did on Malta.

The heat of high summer was declining and the weather was becoming more bearable, and the winds were much cooler too, so my blood was raging less than it used to, what with that and age creeping on. Nonetheless I couldn't resist him, he was so fair, and had such a naughty smile. It was his skin I think that ensnared me more than anything. It was pale and soft, his cheek was quite beardless, but he had a fringe of blonde hair down his forearms and across the small of his back. Nor was he was innocent. He knew how to give and take his pleasures already. Alof didn't make him his personal pageboy for nothing.

I didn't tell you that about Alof, did I? Well, nobody knows about it, and just as well, for he would be burned alive and bring shame and ignominy on the Order if it were suspected. How do I know? Well, I can see my own kind when they stand in front of me, can't I? You can see a horse when it's coming.

The boy liked it too. He was facing a possible future of celibacy, and had not yet tried women, partly he said for fear of coming to like them too much and then be left wondering if he could do without them. He was clever, I knew it when I painted him. And he may have been called a boy, but he was of military age and bearing all right. That much I can testify to. And he needed pleasure, the same as any young man with blood in his veins. So there we are. I give you all of this information not as justification, for you know where I stand on all that. This is just the way it was.

He would get away whenever he could, and come to a room I had been given as a studio and would lie upon a day bed there, which I often used as a prop for my models. And the happiest times were always afterwards, when the late sun shone aslant through the open window and we shared a glass of wine and wondered what the evening would bring. He was so full of life and hope and expectation that my pleasures with him were always tinged with sadness for myself. Past a certain age, no matter in what regard we are held by our fellow men, nor how much they heap praise or riches upon you, you will always know deep down that you are not worthy.

Oh to be young again and loved on a hot afternoon.

Disaster struck one evening as I was returning late from an assignation down in the docks. (Three sailors, a whore, a donkey and a jar of lard, since you ask. My, she was a game lass. Quite how she fitted me in as well I do not know.) I did not go to my quarters, as I always did, but to my studio for no reason at all, but that I was fuddled from drink and exhausted from the other thing.

And even as I approached I heard scrabblings from within and urgent whispers, and as I pushed open the door a figure brushed past me in the dark in a great hurry, but not so quick that I did not get an impression of who he was. I let him go. And inside was the pageboy, Antonino. I lit a lantern and sat with him and he looked more and more wretched. And he did not know where to look or what to think and began to pace. And I told him that it was all right, I am not a jealous man, and if he should seek pleasure elsewhere that was fine by me. I would like still to see him from time to time, I said, for he moved me in such a way which I did not explain, but still, we are all men here, I said, and we must take our pleasures where we must.

He looked at me in horror and told me that I did not understand. That the man who had been here with him was Alof. 'Why, what of it?' I said. 'I knew it was he from his bulk and his smell even as he brushed past me in the door. And I have guessed as much about you and he from the moment I first set eyes on you both for that portrait.'

'Yes,' he said. 'But now Alof knows that you know about

him, which he did not guess before. And he cannot trust you to keep quiet.'

'I will not say a word,' I said. Dear God, how could I have been so naive? No doubt I was still light-headed from all my successes. A knighthood, some good paintings, a lovely boy, naked lust down in the docks just for the asking, and a good distance between me and the Pope; what more could mortal man ask? Well, the Furies came round fast enough after all that pride. And they were treading on my tailbone and breathing fire four-square up my arsehole already and I didn't even have the wit to notice. Sometimes I think I deserve all I get.

No, I don't. No one deserves what I will get.

The *Guva*

I was in prison, and ye came unto me

St Matthew 25: 36

They showed up within an hour and they threw me in the *guva*. No questioning, no declarations of arrest, no trial, nothing. Five thickset knights just came out of the dark, grabbed me, bound my hands, hauled me off to the dungeon and lowered me on a rope. Antonino screamed, just once, briefly and not very loud, and I told him quite sharply to be quiet and say nothing, for then they could prove nothing. 'And go to Alof, and salvage what you can,' I said over my shoulder as they took me away. Poor boy, he is caught in the middle. I cannot blame him if he cleaves to Alof. He is the most powerful man here, and has the boy's future, indeed the boy's very life, in the palm of his hand.

Mine too, now I think about it. And believe me, there is plenty of time to think down here. Ooooh, fuck.

This place is not nice. I could see where they were bringing me when they hauled me off. To the Castle, which stands at the mouth of the harbour and has been most

176

useful as a fort to the Order in the past. It was built bang on top of an already existing castle, and it was from here that the grand master and all his hundreds of knights had fended off the Turk bastards I told you about. It was yellowish in colour because built of sandstone, not that I could see what colour it was at all that night. It might have been the colour of the Devil's turds for all I cared. I had been round it before, conducted regally when I got my K, by the same knight who kept me company on the boat. But he hadn't shown me the *guva*.

Way down at the bottom of the castle there was a hole in the flagstones of the basement. It was about as wide as a man's shoulders, which was just about right, because what they did was pass a rope under my arms and lower me into the hole. Fuck me, I was sweating I can tell you. At first I thought perhaps the sea lay below, and I was about to be given a watery grave in very short order, but I could hear no waves, and anyway they had not bound my wrists. Then I thought that perhaps there were wild beasts, and I was to be fed to them. Then I thought of all sorts of instruments of torture, being oiled and cranked up in preparation for me. And I was wrong on all counts. There was nothing. And that was the worst torture of all.

I landed on the ground in a heap, and they withdrew the rope up after me, and shut the hole. No light at all, not even darkness visible. This is the worst I can imagine, my eyes wide open, and nothing, nothing can I see. Now I know what it is to be blind. And I will go mad very soon, I know it, if there be no light come to me soon.

For my eyes are everything to me. I live in my eyes, and if my eyes be dead, then I am dead too even though I may be breathing. I will go mad, I feel it coming on.

I do not know how long it was, it must have been all night, say some six hours no more, but for me it was half my lifetime. I had to keep firm hold of my mind. I rubbed and chaffed my wrists against the wall, and used pain to prove to my mind that I was alive and not mad. At least the pain was real. And I was careful not to hurt my hands, in case I might use them to escape later. Just that small thought kept me going through the night and kept me sane. Also the faint scuffling sounds of the rats. They were a great comfort to me. I have no fear of rats. I have come to know them and their ways over the years from my stays in prison. They are not to be feared. Indeed, they behave better than most men.

Finally, after dawn, some little light began to filter in and illumine the chamber. I know not where from, for there was no window, but it came from above, and crept across the walls, so there must have been some slight opening higher up, which funnelled in this tiny amount of the sun, it was hardly more than a candle some half a mile away in a storm. But it was enough to keep me from madness. For at last I could see where I was and so could build upon the picture.

Some previous incumbent had scratched a sketch on the wall of a funeral hearse, complete with six black-plumed horses and his name on the side of the hearse, although it was too scuffed for me to read. The picture was not well done, sketched bluff, or four-square, head-on to the viewer with no attempt at perspective. And there were no cross-hatchings or shadings to suggest mass or bulk. Nor any human figures in it such as a driver or mourner. I'd have been ashamed to leave a memory such as that behind me. So much for the notion that death concentrates the mind; it does not. Nor does it turn you into any sort of an artist.

This dungeon was bell-shaped, with the opening at the top up at the point from which the bell would be hung. The floor was beaten earth and solid. I could not dig it with my fingernails. And the walls curved away upwards toward the trap some thirty feet above. They were completely smooth and concave so that, even if there had been handholds at regular intervals, you still could not scale them, for your weight would simply drop you back to the floor. And break your leg into the bargain. Not that anyone would notice.

They left me there five days, I counted them off. But I did not mind so much as that first night when I could not see. Once I had the measure of where I was, then I could construct castles in my mind. And so I did, building great palazzi brick by brick, just as I had watched my father do when I was a boy; albeit not palazzi, but little outbuildings on a smaller scale. And that was just one trick to pass the time. I thought of other things too. Oh, I tell you, when my mood is right, there is hardly a day goes by when I don't have some thought or other come into my mind.

I had been in prison before, and while it was never so terrible as this one, still I knew the score. And I knew how to measure out the time in parcels and kill it slowly. The worst fate would be not knowing how long they would be keeping you inside. But I knew they would have to come for me sooner rather than later. No more than five or six days, because I was going to have to be dealt with while still upright and strong. That much I had worked out.

Alof, it seemed to me, was going to have to deal with me privately but distantly. It were no good murdering me here in the dark, for too many people knew of my presence here. There was the pageboy, of course, and then at least those five knights who bundled me here, not to mention any number of turnkeys, for I had lost count as I was frogmarched in.

He could leave me here to rot, or he could have me garroted quietly by one of his hired thugs, but that sort of thing gets around and people would very soon be asking awkward questions about that nice new knight we saw invested recently at that lovely ceremony and what on earth had become of him. So I would have to be dealt with, fatally for preference, somewhere else, somewhere off the island. And first I must be seen to have left the island, and in some sort of disgrace, so that not too many questions be left hanging in the air.

Now how would he do that? For he could not possibly bring me to trial, for fear I might accuse him in public of the unnatural act that I had witnessed between him and his lovely blond pageboy. (Ah, the thought of him and his long, small arms helped through several of the nights in that hole.) Yet he must eject me from the place in some disgrace. It seemed to me that there were several possibilities, but whatever else might come, I would be out within six days.

Five, as it turned out. I was asleep on the floor when I heard the trap open above me, and a strong shaft of light flooded in, blinding me for some moments. Then I heard a voice in a powerful whisper. It was Antonino, the pageboy.

And he threw me down a rope ladder, and I climbed up it, albeit shakily, for I was unfed and still stiff from the floor. And God bless the boy, he had brought me bread and water and some fruit and olives bundled in his cloak, which I wolfed down while he gabbled on. I did not hear him too clearly, but the gist was that while he had come here of his own accord, Alof had already hinted that he should come to me and er . . . 'comfort' me. Alof had been vague, but left the boy in no doubt as to when the guards might be looking in the opposite direction.

Poor boy, I understood all right what was happening, indeed I was way ahead of him. Alof was using him to get under way my escape from the island, but in such a way that he could deny all knowledge after the event, and if necessary accuse the boy of complicity and have him . . . I was about to say put on trial, but good God that would mean a possible death sentence.

No, upon reflection, I think the boy will be all right. Alof is clearly fond of him, and will contrive to shield him. What I have to do now is leg it as fast as my wobbly legs will carry me. And the boy led me in the right direction, clear across the main courtyard in bright moonlight, all the while reassuring me that none would see. Which they did not. And then he lowered me down a couple of twenty-foot walls, with the aid of the rope ladder which he was still carrying, coiled around his shoulders. And still there was no warning shout from any of the garrison sentries. Alof must have spent a lot of bribe money that night. Or spiked their drinks.

Or perhaps he had taken the five knights who had arrested me into his confidence, and told them of a terrible crime that I had committed that would bring the Order into disrepute, and so for the sakes of all our reputations, they must stay blind and mute and let me escape off the island and into oblivion for ever.

Except . . .

My brain was now running on quite fast, and I did think perhaps I was delirious from the stay in gaol, but I examined my thoughts and my self quite carefully, and I think I was whole and sane . . . except that once off the island, I would talk. I had no reason to stay silent. People would ask why I had left Malta after only a short while, and I had no reason not to tell them the truth. At least, that is how Alof would see it. No one stays silent for long, and word gets around.

So, I may get away, but from now on I will be hounded. One of those five knights, perhaps all of them, will be given special dispensation for a murder, and they will follow wherever I go, and that murder will be mine. I must be silenced, but well away from Malta, with no hint of treachery on the part of the sainted knights, God rot the lot of them. And to think I wanted to be one!

I must think of a plan. The boy and I were now quite free of the garrison, and running toward the harbour, hugging the walls, but not very ostentatiously, for it did not much matter now if the locals saw us.

He got a hold on my sleeve and tugged me on and round a corner, and there we were, with a ship, quite large, right bang on the opposite kerb of the street. It's a funny harbour in that respect. It looks like any other city, with streets and buildings, yet you turn a corner, and there is an enormous boat, seemingly parked in a gap in the houses.

It was still dark, so there was not any activity on board, but there was a watch posted at the top of the gangway, and the boy duly approached him and had words that I could hear muttered. I followed him up the plank in some trepidation, but could soon see that all was well. It was a galley, and I could see by its cut that it belonged to Colonna, the very family that had brought me to Malta in the first place. So here I was back again, it might even have been the very same boat.

The boy bid his farewell to the night watch, and passed him a purse which clinked, and then turned at the top of the plank, I think to say his farewells. But I would not allow it. I bundled him down the gangway and into a dark corner at the back of the dock, and put my arm around him and embraced him most tenderly, and he me.

And I asked more questions about who had put him up to all this, but he shook his head and looked away, and could not speak. Poor boy. He was but a pawn, and he felt he was betraying me, but could do nothing. I reassured him that all would be well with me. I had my sword and my dagger (he had brought both to me, good boy) and with those about me and a little money I could make my way in the world wheresoever I pitched up. And he would be safe if he just did what Alof told him or hinted to him. He should not worry about betraying me at all. God knows my reputation is bad enough. He cannot do me more harm, and indeed he has more than acquitted any debt to me by this night's actions. Kind boy, good boy; now go home and sleep and may fate give you a life of simpler decisions in the future.

Though it won't, for fate is a bitch. So take this as a lesson and learn from it, boy. The best of intentions are turned to ashes in the mouth by a malign fate. And humans too.

But that last is nothing that a dagger on a dark night can't cure. Which is why I have mine about me at all times, as I have told you, even while I sleep. Mark that well too, boy. Horrid as it seems to you now, there are men who would not hesitate to use one on you. Beware the world, my boy, and the men in it. You look kindly upon it now, but the bloom of it wears thin after but a few summers.

Life for me will be tough from now on. They will all be after me now, the Pope's lot, the knights' lot and God knows who else besides. Well, such is life. Only women and children cry when the world doesn't go their way. I will do what I always do. Stand up straight and face the front.

Freedom, then Sicily

Dazzled thus with height of place,
Whilst our hopes our wits beguile,
No man marks the narrow space
Twixt a prison and a smile.

Henry Wotton. 'Upon the Sudden Restraint
of the Earl of Somerset'. 1651

And so I was free. I wasn't even seasick on the voyage. The galley men heaved and creaked at their oars, the vessel puffed her sail, and the dark broad seas gloomed at me, as they always do, but I was happy as a twirling dervish. No more Malta for me, that nasty little enclave of sex-crazed perverts. I wanted a clean slate in a new, fresh-minted sort of place with boundless horizons, where men could go about their affairs without fear of being robbed or killed for their money or their beliefs. Where the towns were ruled by honest officials, and one did not have to bribe or buy justice. Where a man might be safe from bandit and priest alike.

So, they dropped me in Sicily.

Truly fate is an ironist.

Minitti took me in, hurrah for Minitti. I knew he had returned to Syracuse at breakneck speed, after our run-in with Ranuccio in Rome, and the authorities marking him down as not just a valuable eyewitness but a potential murderer too. For Syracuse was where he was born, and he always had it at the back of his mind as the place to retire to anyway. Quite how he had got wind of me arriving I did not know, but then Syracuse is an open port, separated from Valetta by only a short stretch of water. Word travels fast among sailors. Anyway, there he was, waving on the quayside and hugged me like a bear when I slouched off the ship, and slapped my back like an old dog, and he took me into his house and made me a bed, even though his wife did give me the evil eye at first. No doubt my reputation precedes me. So I was as quiet and as polite as I knew how, which as you will guess was tough going. No doubt she thinks I will take Minitti off whoring. Well, maybe I will. It would do the poor pussy-whipped bastard a bit of good. Let a woman in your life, and your fun days are through.

So, after a day or two to reassure the old trout, I took him off one afternoon, and we started drinking a little early for me, but still it set us going, and once off I knew he would not want to return for the rest of the evening. And it was a good evening, talking of old times in Rome, and the way we left it in such a hurry. He had written to Ranuccio's family, the Tomassoni clan, and appealed to them for pardon, a necessary first step in law to avoid the court's penalties.

But he had heard nothing. And like as not to, ever after, I told him. The Tomassonis were bastards to a man, and would hold a grudge until doomsday. Never mind that Ranuccio was an unblooded little twerp, all prick and bones, and a pimp to boot, he was one of their own; and so their ridiculous notions of 'honour' demanded blood for blood. Never mind that the Tomassoni family hadn't done an honourable thing in six generations, unless you count butchering Huguenots, which no doubt puts them on the list of the Pope's 'honourable' men. Never mind that they would kill men for the highest bidder.

(My father had told me that he could remember a special service in Milan in which a letter from the Pope was read out declaring his overwhelming joy at that massacre in Paris which all but wiped out the Protestants. Ah Jesus, the God of mercy.)

'So,' I said to little Minitti, 'forget the Tomassonis and fuck 'em. Here's wine to wash away your cares, then we'll to cunt again.'

He looked over his shoulder at that suggestion, then looked a bit sheepish, then slowly a budding grin swept across those chubby little cheeks of his, till he was like a great big fat happy baby. It never fails, that word.

So we shared a whore, which gave me another chance to look at Minitti on the job again, and I was surprised that my ancient lust for him which was never requited had quite gone. Anyway middle age is creeping on him, and he is quite fat around the middle. Not me, though, which is hardly surprising. You try living in a dungeon for six days, with no food and the prospect of a hanging. It's a good way to stay lean.

The whore was good, and since I did not want any more clap just yet, I was scared of the mercury, I just got a hand-job from her, and she had kind hands. I lay back and found myself dwelling on Fillide's face. It was Minitti's presence brought her to mind. It is strange, but she is the first person that I have ever had a strange yearning for, once we have been separated. Usually, when a person bids farewell, they are out of my mind completely until we meet again. Indeed, it is as if they have died as far as I am concerned. I never turn my mind to an absent one.

But Fillide's face swam into my mind's eye, just as surely as if she had called out my name beneath the open window. And I do not know quite what to make of it. At least I can use her face again in my picture without having to pay her to stand there. There is that in its favour. But why does she come to me, and trouble me so? I never promised her much. Unless you count immortality, of course. That is not much, perhaps, but it's all that heaven allows.

I came to, out of my reverie, without even noticing that I had come, which is surely unusual, isn't it? Isn't it? Have you ever done that? I never have, till now. Most odd. I was so turned around in my brain that I paid the whore again, forgetting that I had paid her beforehand, though she said nothing of course. And Minitti and I staggered out into the moonlight.

It was an odd main square in this town, not really a square at all, but a sort of oblong ellipse, of the sort I can draw with a oversize circle of string set between two pins at less of a distance than the diameter of the circle. If you follow me. No geometry in your schooling? Well, picture a partially inflated tubular bladder. It is a good space, though, well proportioned and well thought-out by the man who originally laid it.

And the buildings are pleasing and all of a piece with the piazza. I thought that I could come to like this town, until a couple of days later I realized that you could explore every nook and cranny in it in less than a day or so. I suspect its geometry derives from the curious shape of the city itself. It sticks out into the sea like a knob on a door.

And it goes back a long way, having been a Greek settlement at one point. It was even supposed to be their biggest city outside Athens, so they say at any rate. But it's still very small. And that worried me more than somewhat. It has too many dark corners for my liking.

There is a freshwater spring, which comes bubbling out of the ground right near the saltwater shoreline down by the harbour. Which is a strange thing, but makes it very useful to passing ships, which need to take on new barrels of drinking water. They scarce have to send men for it, but just lift it straight from spring onto ship. But that very convenience makes for rather too much traffic for my taste. Every ship which heaves over the horizon causes me to hunch up a little, and look for a quick way out of wherever I am, in alley or tavern, for it might contain one of those big bruiser Knights of Malta. Or even all five of them.

Not that I couldn't deal with one or two of them, I've done that before after all. But it would get my blood up again, and I don't want that, not now. I've still the murder from Rome on my head, not to mention the unmention able from Malta, so another murder would not look too good if ever the judges ask to see my record sheet.

Lucy and the Mighty Arse

Or to some coffee-house I stray
For news, the manna of the day.

Matthew Green. 'The Spleen'. 1737

Minitti got me a commission, God bless his little breeches
thrice over. He has set up a workshop here, and has at least
a dozen apprentices all turning out hack work which he
himself signs. I think it a mistake, for some of it is very bad,
and so he does his reputation a disservice. But still it makes
him a lot of money and he is very popular with the general
public, especially with his still lifes of flowers and his young
courting couples in love. And nothing wrong with that at all,
I say; while privately making a mental note that he is a crap
painter. But never mind. Everyone needs a friend they feel
superior to. The same goes for a woman too. You wouldn't
want a wife who thought herself your superior, now would
you? That would be intolerable.

Anyway, he knows all the right people here on the island
and they all think he is a true gentleman, which he is in his
way. And he got me introduced to one of the Senate, and

it seemed they wanted a *Burial of St Lucy*, not a saint I know much about, not that I give a fuck for any of the saints, of course, but I need something of her character to help me work it all out. And they didn't know much about her either.

Well, I need the money badly, and so I said yes, and set to work, very fast, much faster than I usually do, and even did not use much by way of models, but rather painting much of it from memory, for the first time in my life. It was the strange vision of Fillide that did it. She haunts me, and I used her features, albeit botched and disguised slightly, for Lucy. This is the first time I have used my memory rather than life, and if nothing else, I can get it done even faster than usual.

I like the name Lucy. I have never had a woman called Lucy, and I would like to, just because I like that name, I know not why. In Latin it means 'light'. No doubt you know that, but I did not till Minitti told me. As I have told you, I am not well lettered in any language.

She is the local saint of the town. According to a copy of *The Golden Legend*, which the priest dusted off and referred to, it seems she wouldn't put out her virginity for the man to whom she was betrothed, the mean bitch, and so he denounced her to the authorities as a Christian, which in those days was as good a way as any of getting rid of people who had irked you. They did her in, although accounts vary as to how exactly. The story I liked best, which I got from the priest of the church where it was to hang as altarpiece, was that she had her throat cut after some brawl with a local consul from Rome. Sounds like a game girl to me.

They buried her down in the catacombs, so I painted her stretched out in the earth, her hand out-thrown in a pathetic gesture toward the viewer. And I cut her head off from her neck, which I had not done in a little while, not even in the *Beheading of St John* back in Malta.

It gave me bad dreams, such as I get for much of the time nowadays, and I do not like them, being fond of my sleep. It makes me drink even more of an evening, just to get a decent sleep, but then I am not fit for work in the morning and that can often be no good, with a deadline looming, or else those knights galloping over the horizon at a hundred miles an hour. So no more nights out on the drink, and fewer nightmares of headless corpses if you please. So went back, just as I once had done for the *Assassination of St Matthew*, and I painted over the severed neck and rejoined her head to her body and painted a scarf wrapped around her neck where once the bloody gap was. I slept better after that. And the priest liked it better too, not that I give a toss about what he likes or doesn't.

And then I painted in a group of bystanders all around the body, all jostling for a look at the corpse, including the priest, looking like a chinless wonder. And finished that lot, and stepped back and reached for my rag to wipe my brush, as I like to do, and I looked at my picture and nearly died from boredom there and then. God, it was crasher.

I'd had that problem with portraying Jesus often enough, he's always about as interesting as watching plaster dry. But I had never had that trouble in other subjects. I could see what it was. No one on the picture was doing anything, except gape at the body. I needed action, I needed drama, I needed something to draw you in to the picture. So I threw a length of sacking over the easel, which was in place in the church, since I had not yet got a studio. And I went out into the piazza and sat down outside a bar and had an espresso and a cigarette just as the sun was declining, and shooting its burning ray oblique between the buildings, which set up nice shadows, the way I like them, and a haunting, lambent light.

Sorry about that, I hate it when people bang on about the quality of the light. Especially writers of fiction. It was a very quiet late afternoon, just a faint hiss from a distant fountain and the muted skitter of lizards on the walls. Some men were digging up one corner of the square, lifting some worn-out cobbles and then pegging out straight lines with nails and string, and tamping down wet sand before laying new cobbles. It was intricate work, as well as quite back-breaking, and I became absorbed in watching the patterns they created with the stones. They were bent double over their work most of the time. And sweating heavily but absorbed by what they did, and not at all bored.

I am sure you can see the way I am going.

I did not sketch them but looked longer and harder than

I did before when I was just idling over my coffee. And then I went back the next morning to look at them again, before returning to my picture.

And in front of St Lucy, I put in two enormous grave diggers. Huge burly men, just like the pair out in the square, with beards and shaved heads, sweating away in their underwear with their shovels, bang in front of the body and framing her neatly by their diagonal bodies, and blotting out some of those boring onlookers. And the light is coming in from the right, high up, as usual, and it shines direct on one gravedigger's loincloth and highlights his enormous arse. Just like that horse in *St Paul on the Road to Damascus* I did all those years ago. That should enrage the priests, not to mention the Senate.

Not a word was said. But I got a feeling of polite shuffling of feet. That is how it is with provincials. The word had got around that I was one of Rome's best, and they didn't like to contradict it. At least I think that was it. Maybe they know something I don't. Maybe they've seen in the distance over my shoulder a ship on the horizon and don't like to frighten me. Oh, you can see how much troubled I am, my thoughts always come back to that. Well, so would yours.

Messina

All good writing is swimming under water and holding your breath

F. Scott Fitzgerald. Letter to his daughter. 1962

I finished it, I got my money, and I said I was sorry to Minitti but I just could not settle down in Syracuse. It was that great big open harbour staring across the water to Malta just over the horizon. It was beginning to look like an open road, just asking to be filled with a posse cantering along it, all hell-bent on revenge. It began to trouble me so, that again I could not sleep, but would lie on my bed all night, fully clothed with my dagger in my belt and my sword beside the bed. And in the mornings I felt foolish to be so frightened like a child. But not at four in the morning I didn't, I can tell you. So it was up early and put a little bread and water in my knapsack, and thank you Mrs Minitti for having me and yes, I will see you all again soon. But I knew I would not.

There was Palermo, the capital of the island to the north-west. Or there was Messina to the north-east, a bigger town than Palermo strangely enough, for it was a thriving seaport, and the nearest one to the mainland of Italy, which was just a short stone's throw over the Straits of Messina. Men have even talked of building a bridge over the straits, though none can do it yet, for they have not the means. It would be the longest in the world, I think. Men have certainly swum it, though the currents can be treacherous.

You can see from my description that I chose Messina first. Really it was a toss-up. In fact quite literally a toss-up, for I was so much indifferent that I threw a coin in the air and it came down heads, which meant Palermo.

So I went to Messina instead, because I'm fucked if I am going to be ruled by superstition.

But first, by way of a little diversion, Minitti took me along the coast to little fishing village called Selinunte, and he taught me to swim. Well, there's a thing. I'll bet you never thought I would be able to swim. Not many people can.

Selinunte cannot number more than a hundred souls, all huddled around in some rude dwellings close to the beach. They are a crude folk, heavily tanned from going out in their boats, but friendly.

And behind their small beach settlement lies an enormous number of strange ruins, left by the Greeks before our age, which the locals leave alone, save as a handy source for some bits of stone, when they need a new fireplace, or such. You can wander the streets of this one-time town, and see the foundations of the walls of the houses, and very small and poky they must have been, and with the alleyways between the houses very narrow.

But behind the ruined houses lie glories. Four beautiful temples, made of pure marble, which shine in the moonlight and are of such proportion as to move one to tears. I do not know to what God the ancient Greeks prayed, but they must have prized Him more highly than we do ours. Our churches are wretched things compared to these. That is one thing that we could do well to learn. I have seen what the Roman Emperors did in Rome, and it is true that the Pantheon and the Tivoli are impressive. And of course I have seen our modern churches, some of which are good. But nowhere near do they get to the glories of the Grecian temple.

We went into the sea in the late afternoon, when the sun had declined from its highest burning, and Minitti borrowed a horse, for a small payment, which the locals use to haul the boats up the beach. And we took the horse into the sea with us, and I clung to the mane, while Minitti swam alongside me, encouraging me to strike out on my own. But I could not, I was very fearful, and, as I have said before, I do not like the water. You cannot breathe in it for one thing.

So on our second attempt Minitti persuaded me to dunk my head under water and open my eyes. And what a scene was there! For the first time since being a child, I was looking at a world brand new. There was the horse, floating quite serenely on the surface, and down beneath its legs were pumping back and forth in a steady rhythm, as if it were doing a gallop but in slow motion, as in a dream. It was lovely. And there were fishes of all colours, which I did not like at first, since for all I knew they would bite me. And slimy things that I steered clear of.

After that, swimming came quite easy. I don't say I lost my fear of the deep, but I did at least become acquainted with it, and knew what I could do in it, and what I could not. To swim, I simply floated, then thrashed my arms and legs about like a frog. Not very elegant, but it may save me from a sinking boat, you never know. But it is underwater I like best, when the sun's rays illumine the caves and coral and grottoes so that it seems like a fairyland. I could not paint it. It is too fantastical for men to believe.

None of the fishermen could quite believe what we were doing, but stood watching us with their jaws open. It has never occurred to them to swim. Actually we spoke to them over a supper of lobsterfish, and they confided that they would regard it as tempting fate, or rather tempting the god of the sea, for I think they are secretly a pagan lot, although they keep silent on that score. Very wise, you never know when those Inquisition bastards will come sticking their twitchy little noses in your business. I told them that, and they laughed. If they learned how to escape from the sea-god's clutches, they said, he might be tempted to test them more by conjuring up storms and sinking their boats, for his amusement. And they didn't want that. It has its own kind of logic, I suppose.

After a couple of days frolicking in the spume we returned to Syracuse and I set out for Messina, as I told you. It took me a while to reach that city, for it was bandit country I traversed. I travelled by night mainly, when the roads were empty, so I was more safe. My night vision is good. By day I slept where I could, usually in barns or haystacks. And once in another old Greek temple, which was ruined though very lovely in its proportions. Especially the columns. My father had taught me about them, and how they were shaped with a bulge just a third of the way up, to give them elasticity, as if they were flexing their knees from the weight of the roof. And indeed that is exactly how they were, and they were soothing to look at, as if the builders knew that they had got it all, all of it, absolutely just so.

I get that sometimes after a painting. Not always, though, and not lately. With St Lucy I really wasn't at my best. Too fast, too ill thought out, no live models or hardly any if you include the diggers. Oh, I can still do it all, one hand tied behind me, standing on my head, but I wonder if will ever be satisfied again. As wholly pleased with my efforts as when I did the *Beheading of St John* in Malta. I would have been happy to go out in style after that one picture. But there was life left still in me, and as long as there is life I must keep painting. What else can I do?

One day, on the road, I became uneasy. I paused under

a tree beside a stream, but there was too much noise from the bubbling water, so I moved away, further in among the trees, but again the wind was rustling the leaves and gave out too much noise, so I went beyond the copse, and waited. I opened my mouth, because this always seems to help me hear better. I do not know why, but an open mouth seems to operate like a third ear for me. My hearing is not so acute these days.

Some noise came to me on the wind, I am sure of it. It was only a slight noise, and so I do not think it be a gang of *banditi*, for they are a rough lot and travel in packs and do not much care how much noise they make. You can hear them coming around a mountain a mile away. This noise was just a gentle sigh, like a horse blowing through its nose or a man settling in a chair. I waited but could not see anything in the distance and so set off again.

But I could not shake off the feeling that I was being watched from behind. It is strange, but I always know when someone is looking at me. It is not a conscious thing. I can be sitting in a quiet tavern, minding my own business, and suddenly, for no reason, I will turn around, and there will be someone over by the wall or in a corner, watching me. One glance from me and they tend to avert their gaze, and more often than not they will make the sign to avert the evil eye. I know what I look like, so I don't blame them. Indeed it was probably my very ugliness that caused them to stare in the first place. But, always, upon reflection afterwards, I cannot recall registering any feeling that I was being watched until I turned around and confirmed it. Somehow, the watcher must have conveyed his actions to a part of my brain which was not conscious. I am sure that animals do it all the time. Just watch a deer grazing.

But this time, out in the badlands of eastern Sicily, I often paused and scanned the horizon behind me, but could see nothing. The hairs on the nape of my neck still prickled though from time to time. And I knew my hairs could be trusted. So I forged ahead, making good time, and would be in Messina quite soon, where I could find out who was following easily and kill him if needs be. Out in the country-side I am lost.

When I could see the edges of Messina, and the wall it had about it, though the entry gate was not yet distinct, I turned once more, and there, no mistake this time, I saw a glint on the horizon. It was too bright to be metal, such as a piece of armour or a sword. It must have been a mirror or a spy-glass. No one would be using a mirror out in the open. Ergo, it must be a telescope. I had forgotten about those things. Young Galileo had given one to Cardinal del Monte some years ago when I was in his household, as I think I told you, when it was barely invented, and he was using it to survey the movements of the planets and the stars, albeit clandestinely. I took it apart and used the lenses for my own purposes, which were to do with painting, but which are a professional secret and need not concern you anyway.

So out there, at my back, somewhere way over on the horizon, is someone spying on me with a telescope.

I entered the town, a huge place easily as big as Rome, and I headed for the harbour, which I found teeming with sailors, slavers, whores, cut-throats, bandy-legged sluts and the scum of four continents. My kind of place.

I found a cheap room in a smoky tavern, paid for a couple of days in advance, and then vacated it by the window, and found somewhere else, even more anonymous, but with a window overlooking the first place I had paid for. I will sit and watch and see who comes making enquiries. I sat there a whole day. Nobody, not even a blind beggar, arrived at the inn who wasn't a regular. No one looking about them from side to side, no one with their cloak gathered over their face, no shifty Bulgars, no cowardly Lascars, no beady-eyed Serbs, no one who looked like an agent of the Vatican (and what do they look like, I wonder?). I grew impatient and got up and wandered around the town. It was a fearsome, lawless place, far more so even than Rome. The Spanish rule Sicily and the island is the only place in Italy where the Spanish Inquisition have jurisdiction, a fact which means that there is very little constipation among Sicilian natives.

Not in Messina they don't though. It's rich enough and big enough and so teeming with all sorts of life for it to be virtually ungovernable and so is independent of the rest of the island. If the Spanish Inquisition came sniffing round here, they'd get their throats cut and their tongues pulled out through the hole in their neck and then their bodies hung out to dry for the gulls to eat. And that I would dearly love to see.

I was still loafing around down by the harbour on the second day, keeping half an eye out for anyone who might be following me, when I got that old familiar danger signal on the back of my neck. I turned in my chair to face the quayside, and there was Minitti. Good grief, it was only a few days ago I bid farewell to him, and now here he is back, he must have taken a boat around the island. Well, I'm not sorry to see him, though he does look a bit rueful. Can it be him who is spying on me? Surely not, he is a simple boy. Or at least he was when I first knew him. What has he turned into these days? Have the Jesuits got at him? Or the Inquisition? God's boots, I hope not.

Anyway he settled down, placed his pack at my feet and called for a drink. It seemed his wife was acting up again, whining and moaning about me turning up out of the blue and what a bad influence I was, all of which is true enough, though no excuse for any woman to start whining. I mean, they know what I'm like, don't they? Do they think that nagging will somehow make me change my personality?

So Minitti gave her a swift slap to the face and told her he couldn't stand her any more and was off. After which she became remarkably subdued and stopped the incessant complaining. So Minitti took off anyway. Well done, Minitti, you have come a long way from the innocent boy I used to know. His trip to the brothel with me had got his juices going again, and he wanted a bit of the wild life back that we used to enjoy. So here he was, and what should we do?

Lazarus was Dead

'No painter ever painted his own mind so forcibly.'

Henry Fuseli on Caravaggio. 1801

After a few days of nonstop debauchery, the usual de-
pravities, I won't bore you with the details, you can imagine
what we got up to and then multiply it by ten, we slowed our
pace slightly and realized that I would have to find work.
Minitti knew of a man, he always does. I sometimes think he
is better connected than a Pope's nephew.

His name was de' Lazzari, and he was a filthy rich
Genoese who trades in stuff, I know not what. This place is
full of foreigners of his kind. And of course he wanted a
Madonna being adored by St John, because his name was
Giovanni, or because he worked for the Order of St John, or
some such idiot sentiment. I was about to tell him to fuck off,
but Minitti seized his arm and began to flatter and cajole, and
talk him around, he is terribly good at all that stuff, no doubt
that is how he is wealthy.

I just can't be arsed. They can have what I give them
and like it. And just then I did get an inspiration, I thought

about his surname and it was obvious really. And I cut across what Minitti was drivelling to him, and said, 'What about a Raising of Lazarus.' And a look of fantastic vanity and happiness crossed his face, which he quickly tried to cover with one of pious humility, and I knew I had him.

I demanded a fee, which was about double what I used to get, and also a room in the hospital, the one which belonged to his order's church, which I would use as a studio. Both were forthcoming in quick order, so he must have been a very wealthy merchant indeed, although he did wonder aloud why I needed a room in the hospital. I did not tell him what I had in mind. I must do more for the mercantile classes instead of for the Church. They are more easily flattered and less inclined to argue.

It was a good room, clean and airy, swept of dust that very morning, with freshly laundered sheets on the bed which they cleared away into a corner, and an easel ready for me in the centre, and the window open with the light streaming in, which as you will guess I will close before starting. The porters were hanging around at the door, under orders from de' Lazzari, waiting to see if I wanted anything more.

And I told them to get me a fresh corpse.

They looked at each other and cleared their throats a bit and were all about to get up on their high horse, when Lazzari gave a great gulp and his eyes bulged like he's swallowed a frog, but then he told them to get on with it.

There was a pauper of no family who had been buried in an unmarked grave about three days ago. It was the best they could do, not wishing to disturb any other corpse which might have a family attached who might raise a fuss.

So they dug him up there and then, and after I had arranged the room to my liking, with my usual single light source, you know the score by now, I arranged a couple of the beefier porters to hold the stiff so that he was leaning diagonally, with feet on the floor, and head about three feet off the ground.

I don't know when rigor mortis wears off, but he was a bit limp by then, so I got one of the porters to crouch hidden behind the body and hold its right arm up into the air, not quite vertical, to form a sort of cross with the left arm which was hanging floorwards.

And I went to the corpse and opened his eyelids, for I wanted to show a bit of life in the risen Lazarus, but the eyes were rotting and looked like cloudy jellies and had no colour. Never mind, for I could fake that. I left the lids open, though, so I could get the creases and lashes right. Only from life, only from life.

For Lazarus's sister Martha I took one the nuns of the hospital and bid her bend her face close to his, never mind about your expression, I will do that later. I put her in a dark red shift, not a colour I use much these days, and then dismissed her back to her duties, for she was most uncomfortable posing, since she considered the work close to being a whore, never mind the devotional nature of the subject. And in a way she is quite right, the silly old hen, I only used her for a few minutes, just to get the posture right, I can do the face from my memory of Fillide, the whore. Why does she come to me still, I wish she would let me rest in peace, like old Lazarus here? Still there wasn't even any rest for him, poor bastard, once Christ decided he would use him for a miracle.

Christ, oh shit, I had nearly forgotten Christ for the picture. Then I realized I hadn't forgotten him at all, just put him out of my mind with disgust at the prospect of having to do him again. He just will not be left out, barging his way into all the pictures, healing this and healing that, and he's like a bore that no one wants at their party, yet they just can't think of a way to keep him out, and they are all too polite to throw him out, and besides, well, he may just prove to be telling the truth and be someone important after all, so we might as well just let him stick around. Ho hum.

I did the same with Christ as I had done in my *Calling of St Matthew* back in the Contarelli chapel in San Luigi of the French in Rome. Do you not remember? I am sure I told you, perhaps not, forgive me, my memory is going again.

He is standing at the edge as if he has just come in the door, and is pointing at the corpse with one finger curled downward slightly, as I have seen the Greeks do when they beckon someone. And the light is coming from over his shoulder, and so mainly illuminates his arm, and just barely grazes across his cheek, so we can see his nice high cheekbones, but not anything of his expression. Good, He is supposed to be a mystery, three in one and one in three, and all that, so let Him be a mystery. Besides what chiefly interests me as usual is the looks on the faces of the bystanders. Baffled, querulous, unsure of what is going on, and half distracted by something else in the distance. Perhaps they are watching a football match, or a fight, or maybe someone coming over the horizon, oh Christ there I go again.

Anyway I didn't put myself in this one, because I was getting a little tired of repeating some of my trademarks. I was a bit ashamed of giving Christ the same old treatment, but then this is Messina, out in the sticks. Poor old de' Lazzari won't have seen the original in Rome, and even if he had, I doubt he would remember it. Most people, especially rich merchants, don't look long or hard at paintings, they just order them by the yard.

Sorry, I am wandering, because I am filling in the tedious bits of earth and tile around the base of the painting. The top half of the picture can all be black, no light at all. Just slap on the tar.

It was a hot afternoon of the second day, and they finally could take no more. The stench from the corpse was appalling and one of the porters had to run to the window and heave his lunch up over the flowerbed. That did it. They dropped the corpse on the floor with a horrible squelch and stood there, mute and defiant, until the leader spoke up and said they would help no more. They stuck their chins up and out at me and were about to walk off, and I was half minded to let them, but then I remembered I was paying them well, and anyway I hadn't finished.

Actually I thought of none of that. What I thought was: no half-witted, shit-faced, counter-jumper of a hospital porter was going to tell me what to do.

So I strode to their leader, and pulled my dagger from under my shirt and had it at his throat before he had even finished his little speech. And I pushed the point into his neck a little, not far, but just enough to raise a little blood in a trickle onto his dirty white collar, and I grabbed his hair by my free hand, turned him slightly so they could see, and I looked at each in turn, still grinding the knife in so he whimpered and breathed through his teeth. And I said nothing.

They returned to their posts, and picked up the corpse and resumed their poses, even the poor bastard at the back who was twisted awkwardly, looking off stage.

And when I had finished for that day, I threw down my brushes and stalked away, leaving them standing there, without dismissal. And a few minutes later, I came back into the room, and do you know they were still all there, posed as stiffly as if they had a poker up their arses.

'Same time tomorrow,' I barked. They relaxed and started to shuffle off, muttering under their breath. 'And we finish when I say we finish,' I shouted, and left again.

The next day they were two short. Apparently both men had been taken into the hospital with a fever, and the others looked fearful. I got them into their pose again, with the stinking cadaver, and held it until midday, and then I had got all I needed and dismissed them. I had it in mind to keep them at it an extra day just to prove my point, but I did not want any more unnecessary deaths on my hands so I let them go. I think they got the message about art. They marched off in short order to put the corpse to bed.

There is no resurrection after death. Only stink and decay and corruption. It's a lie, what the priests tell you.

I had them carry the canvas over to de' Lazzari's house and was to show him the finished thing almost before the oil was dry. But no, he came over all of a dither with excitement, and said he wanted a private showing so that he could impress all his rich merchant friends and also the jolly men of the Order of St John and all the money raisers for the charity and so on. So they propped it up against a wall, it was almost too big for an easel, for I had put a huge amount of black space above the corpse, almost half as much again as the whole painting, for I wanted a cavernous feeling to it, as if Lazarus were floating upward into the darkness of the vault of heaven. And they hung a white sheet over it, with a bit of cord for when they would yank it off.

And the next day de' Lazzari assembled all his friends and relations for a big feast, and before he could even get going with a speech about it and all his good works, someone had pulled at the cord and everyone was crowding around for a good look.

Now the problem is that everyone is a critic. Never mind that they don't know the first thing about painting, wouldn't know one end of a brush from another, and have only seen ten paintings in their life, never mind that they would not know a great painting if a Leonardo jumped up and sank its teeth into their gonads, never mind any of that, they always have an opinion on it.

And do you know, I don't mind if an ignorant man says, 'Oh, I like that,' or 'Oh, that's not to my taste.' I really don't mind that at all.

What I can't stand are the ones who think they know all about it. They use the words like 'sublime' and 'quite awesome' and 'a masterpiece, pure and simple' (as if any human activity were ever pure or ever simple). They chatter on about chiaroscuro and pentimenti as if they were cognoscenti (another word they would use) and then, insult to injury, they will invoke another painter: 'I think his use of light is surpassed only by Bellini himself.' Or 'His figure work is not a patch on Michelangelo, but he has integrity.'

That was how it was with the Lazarus crowd. And, oh God help me, I was never nervous before a final showing to the patron, but that he should turn my painting over to the opinion of this crowd of morons, it was too much. I could feel the blood rising in my head again, and my neck began to swell and the sound in my ears was like an army marching on gravel.

Minitti saw the state I was getting into, and he came to me and put his arm on mine, and had such a look of care about me on him that I almost calmed down. But not quite. I wasn't going to murder one of the sons of bitches, I wouldn't give them that much satisfaction, but by Christ, they weren't going to get away with this. And Minitti saw what I was thinking, and gave a little grin and a giggle and said, 'Go on old Crow, show 'em.'

And I went up to the picture, pushing the crowd of rubber-neckers out of the way, whipped my dagger out from my cummerbund, stuck it into the top left-hand corner and pulled it all the way down to the right, across the canvas. It made a lovely noise.

Silence from the crowd.

So I carried on slashing away, faster and faster, getting all frenzied, not quite foaming at the mouth, although I would have been, given a few more minutes, and ten more yards of canvas, but I soon finished my work, and there was the picture hanging in tattered ribbons, with nothing left whole but the frame (a rather handsome one, carved wood with gesso).

Then I turned and looked at them. 'But we were only praising it,' one of them said aghast.

'There is a certain kind of praise,' I said, 'which only makes me want to go back and start all over again. That sort of praise tells me I have done nothing right.'

I looked at de' Lazzari. His Adam's apple was bobbing up and down and he was almost in tears, poor man.

'I will do this again,' I said to him, softer, but loud enough for the crowd to hear, 'And I will do it better.' I turned and walked away, but could see de' Lazzari perking up a bit from the corner of my eye. Minitti smirking, too. Good.

Two people happy and a lot of idiots who might just think before they speak in future.

Well, of course they won't, I know that, they'll just croak away in their swamp as they always do. But at least it put the wind up them for an hour or two. It's the best you can hope for with arseholes like that.

I was good as my word, I did another canvas for poor old Lazzari, just to show that I did not intend to humiliate him, only his stupid friends, and I did it quick from memory, but this time I did it slightly different. Lazarus is definitely stone dead. Christ may be pointing at him, but the miracle has not begun to work, not yet. The only sign of possible life is his right hand fluttering (maybe, possibly, slightly) up in the black void above them all, where no one can see it because they aren't looking there. As far as the whole entourage is concerned, Lazarus is dead as a nail and Christ has failed. They are all grieving, with not a sign of hope.

I think you can see the state I was in.

The Merchant of Messina

De' Lazzari was not a bad man. I had not had all that much dealing with men of commerce, truth to tell. Most of my dealings for paintings had been with the Church, with one or two exceptions, but I had never really paused to consider the men like de' Lazzari. He was rich beyond all that was ever necessary for his wellbeing. But still he could not rest from making money. I do not understand it. He had enough to retire tomorrow, and keep all his family and relations in some luxury, and still leave a handsome amount in his will. And he could devote himself to his hobbies or his fancies. Catching butterflies, whatever. But he did not. He was troubled by the speculative itch, and it would not let him alone. He just went on piling up riches here on earth.

But he was not a wicked man, as the Bible or at any rate the priests would have you believe about rich men. I do not believe he was bad at all. He might have liked a hard bargain, but he was kind to all that he could be kind to, and I think that is the very best that one can hope for in this life.

And I tell you this. This man was never more innocently employed than when he was making money.

Whether that be profound or not I do not care, but I hold it true.

When I had finished my second canvas for de' Lazzari, we stepped out together and took a little turn around the town, arm in arm, for he liked to show he was a fine fellow, and we were both of us, fine fellows, so he kept saying, and he did truly think so. And we were after our fashion, for I had done him a good picture, I know it is good, and he had given me money. And we were enjoying our *passeggiato*, cutting a fine figure, him in his lovely dark green doublet, and me in my black velvet as usual, wearing a little thin after all my travels, but holding up well. I'll get a new suit soon with the money he gave me.

And we came to a church, and one of his entourage, a local dignitary of some sort, very politely offered me the use of some holy water, which stood at the entrance to the church. And Lazzari looked at me, and said, 'Yes, do, you are still looking somewhat pale and tired from your work.'

And I said, 'What is it good for?'

And they said, 'Why, it will take away all your venal sins before the Lord.'

And I nearly laughed, but it stuck in my craw and came

out like a harsh croak that echoed around the porch, and said, 'That's no use. All my sins are mortal.'

Oh dear. That rather put the cold hand of death on the party. They shook their heads and we wandered off. I didn't mean to be quite so rude. Lazzari took my arm again. 'Never mind, poor man, your brain really is quite troubled, isn't it. Come home with me and rest. We shall look after you.'

A good man, as I said. And surely he will enter the Kingdom of Righteousness just as easily as a poor man. If I have anything to do with it anyway. I'd kill any priest who stood in his way. I'd lay a path to heaven paved with the dead bodies of every priest there has ever been, just so a man like that could get in, riches or no. For he showed me kindness when I had not deserved it. And when a man offers me kindness even in the face of my rude ways, it affects me badly, and my eyes sting a bit. I never knew how to accept a kindness. I had had none in my childhood

I am getting soft in my old age. And it's true my brain is a bit off-key. I am seeing things again. There was a man in black in the square looking at me on the way home. Not just dressed in black like me, but swathed from head to foot in the stuff, with no face, only a black turban where his eyes and nose and mouth should be, but he was watching me I know it. When I looked again, he had vanished. Oh, God, I haven't had visions like that since I was a child and the demons came to talk to me. I need a drink.

I got two bottles of grappa and went to my digs and

drank them down and awoke the next morning with a liver that felt like a punctured football in a muddy *campo*. There were no more visions that night, though, so I don't mind the hangover if that's the price to pay for an untroubled sleep.

I hate dreams. I never have them, or if I do I never remember them. And I do not have them if I drink enough. No more dreams for me, except the ones I can control in the daylight. Daydreams, nothing but daydreams from now on.

I need a nice quiet subject for my next one. My next one? Well, you know me, I cannot rest. I do not know the meaning of the word. It's as if my innards are full to bursting with images. They just come pouring out of me now, like wine from a barrel with a busted spigot. When I was young, it was harder, and I would do any small chore like washing the pots or sweeping the floor to give myself any excuse not to start painting. But now, I can't stop. If I don't walk to that canvas in a morning and address it closely, then my day is a ruin. The whoring and drinking and bad boy stuff of my early days I still need, and will carry on doing, but after I have worked at my colour a while. I never needed any other man's permission for my pleasures, but now I am as old as I am, and a pleasure earned is a pleasure doubled.

So on I went, like a rower beating against the tide and getting nowhere, but unable to stop for fear of being swept away.

The Adoration of the Shepherds

Darkness gave him light.

Henry Fuseli. 1801

The first one I have done to date, strangely, for it is a popular subject. And I am not altogether proud of it, although everyone else seems to be. After Lazarus, word got around, and everyone came to see it, and the local Senate woke up to the fact that the great Caravaggio from Rome was among them, and so they had better get off their arses and do something about it.

So they asked me for a 'Nativity with Shepherds' and so I went to watch a woman giving birth for the first time. That was nasty.

It was down in the docks, not far from the arsenal where they build the ships, in some filthy hovel, that I finally found some poor girl about to drop her child. She was not completely destitute, but only from a poor family, and they welcomed the few *scudi* I gave them and even hired a midwife. I drew the shutters to spare them their neighbours, and watched the delivery. Obviously there was nothing about that which I could use in a picture. Imagine: an altarpiece which showed Mary with her legs apart and a bleeding great child's head pushing its way out of her cunt. That would be something, wouldn't it? God's breath, just the thought of it could get me put away for the rest of my life.

But it was the aftermath I wanted. I wanted to see what Mary and the ageing Father Joseph, the poor old fool looking baffled and still thinking she was a virgin, and the attending shepherds might be doing after it all. And believe me, there was nothing very holy about any of the ghastly business. I have seen so many Nativities in which a radiant Mary holds her son and gazes lovingly into his eyes and holds him aloft from her throne and his halo is all shiny and choirs of attendant angels all sing 'Hosanna' and all the shepherds and the wise men cast their eyes heavenward as if they have all just collectively levitated three feet off the ground.

It's not like that, believe me.

The poor girl was so exhausted she could barely lift her head to look at the baby, and just stared at the floor. The baby for its part was scrabbling around with its pudgy little hands, and probably wanted feeding but didn't know quite where to look for a breast, and the poor girl was too shattered to help it. In fact she was just happy to be alive, for most pregnant women in that part of town die in childbirth.

And the child often dies too, though no one sheds many tears over it, for life does not offer much unless the baby be a healthy boy. And even when it turns out to be a robust, squalling boy, the poor onlookers just stand around wondering what to do, rather than giving thanks to heaven the way the rich and the aristos do whenever they get a son and heir. Only the midwife knew what to do, and I kept her out of the painting. I wanted the little knot of men crouching there bewildered, and wondering what they could do with this newborn thing in their midst.

Thank God the Spanish Inquisition can't get into this town. They'd have my balls if they ever saw this Nativity. I said that to de' Lazzari and he nodded sagely and then later drew me aside and told me with some relish that there is quite a well-run sort of secret organization here, centred in the port, and comprised of quite well-respected men, as well as cut-throats and vagabonds. They see to it that the place is well run, in the interest of their own people rather than the interests of the Church or the rich. They call it a local word, which does not translate too easily, but means roughly 'Our family' or 'Our best interests' something like that. And they certainly look after their own kind too.

The last time the Inquisition came marching in here, they got so badly beaten up at dead of night that they left and never returned. And not just beaten up either. Exactly one half of the priests in the inner circle of that crew vanished off the face of the earth never to be seen again. Not one of their servants or retinue was touched. And no corpse was ever found, nor any evidence anywhere. The head man of the bunch, the Chief Torturer as he would be, considered how best to get justice and wondered whether to call in the troops. He thought about that for a good thirty seconds before realizing that it would involve sending a message by couriers, who would be local men. And then it would be a good day or so before the troops would come marching to the rescue. And so he then did the only sensible thing and fled with all his crew that were still alive. They do say that the fish in the Straits of Messina dined well that night. And that many of the fish that were later caught by the fishermen contained a few holy bits and pieces in their bellies. Rosaries and so on. None were ever turned in to the Church authorities, however.

This secret body, they may be *banditi*, but at least they are our *banditi*. So said de' Lazzari anyway, with a finger to the side of his nose, a gesture which said almost aloud: 'If you ever get in trouble, come and see me.'

Say no more.

My Nativity, then, was simple. No choirs of angels, just a birth in a stable and few old men standing there helpless and the ass looking on without much ado, as if life goes on no matter what, and where's my next mouthful of straw. I reckon it was probably like that in Bethlehem. It certainly was down in the Messina docks, and that means more to me.

I gave the woman more money and wished her well, and

the family saw me out, looking at me like I was some kind of pervert. Which may be true sometimes, but not now, for I did not get aroused by a birth. I just wanted to watch.

That's all I ever do.

The Man with no Face, and a Passion

It belongs not to any mortal that God should speak to him,
except by revelation, or from behind a veil . . .

The Koran. *Sura 42*

I met up with Minitti that afternoon, as we had arranged to
do, me knowing that I would have finished the painting,
him to get away from rushing around meeting possible
clients for the future . . . busy, busy, busy Minitti. Yet he was
not so busy as he would have liked to seem. Something
was troubling him, I could see it. We sauntered past the
arsenal, where they were building some ships, which made
me shudder just to look at, though less so than in the days
before I could swim; and also where a group of children,
just let out of school, were playing. We watched a little as
we walked past and then we settled in a square which Minitti
knew, where he introduced me to one Niccolo, a friend of
de' Lazzari and another merchant. He wanted not one but
four paintings out of me, a cycle of the Passion, no less. I
just nodded and agreed, I am so weary these days that

I agree to everything. Minitti could see this and tried to bargain a little for me, to hike up the price. But I just waved my hand and said, 'No. I'll do it. For whatever price you think fit.'

It was then I saw the figure clad in black again, across the square, looking in my direction. Again, his face was covered, only this time I could see it was like a turban, such as the Moors wear. I started and said something to Minitti, who swivelled to look at the man. He turned back to me with a pitying look. 'It is only an Arab,' he said, 'that is what they wear about their faces to guard against the sand and wind.'

'No. No,' I said, 'he is watching me, I know it, and I cannot see his eyes.' With a sigh, Minitti got up and started to walk briskly towards the figure, but with a swirl of his cloak the man vanished down a side alley. Minitti, who had reached perhaps halfway across the square, returned. I asked if he had seen the man's eyes. 'Yes,' he said, but with some circumspection, and I could see he was puzzled by something. 'How could you see them? I saw nothing. How? What were they like? What colour?' I said. I was shouting now, and only suddenly did I realize that I had gripped Minitti by the jacket, and was twisting the cloth in my clawed hands.

Minitti looked at me strangely and disentangled my hands, with a gentle touch, which calmed me a little. And he said, quite softly, but with an air of disbelief, 'They were pale blue.'

It took me a moment before I saw the full implication of that, I am so slow-witted these days. 'Tell me, oh please do tell me, that there are some Arabs that do have blue eyes,' I said at last.

'I've never seen any,' he said.

I ran the first picture out at my usual speed, and since there was only one figure in it, it was done quick. What can I say? It was good and showed Christ setting off on his journey carrying his cross. That was a subject I could relate to. Christ is seen from the back so I didn't have to show too much of his face. He is clad only in a brown robe, without a crown of thorns, or any other the pious trappings that some painters put in. He is dark-haired, like me, and ragged. His feet are dirty, and he is bent double under the weight of this enormous slab of wood. He is carrying the weight of the world's sin on his shoulders and the indentation on his back is cruel. There is no one else in the painting, no Joseph of Arimathea, no onlookers for once. He just toils on, bereft of all human company, alone on his last journey along a dark street with no visible end.

I cannot finish the cycle. I am going under with some illness, I know not what. I cannot rise in the mornings, and my hands and feet are lead. Nothing arouses my interest, no light, no sign of life, no news, no friend can raise me from my torpor. I am composed of absence and darkness and things which have no life. There is nothing inside me any more. All I do is go through the outward motions of life, like a dead man who won't lie down.

And Minitti is running out of patience, I can see. Well, who wouldn't? I am not much by way of company. I gaze into the far distance mostly and cannot focus on anything to hand. I never did smile much in my life, it is true, but now my face has gone completely slack, and Minitti says I look like a bloodhound. I cannot stand noise, and wince whenever someone shouts nearby. A simple touch on the arm is like being struck by a bunch of nettles and makes me recoil as if stung. I cannot reply to anyone, for I can hardly register what they are saying. Talk is a pain.

I can't go on with my commissioned cycle.

I will go on with it. It's all I can do until this strangeness passes. If I don't do something, anything, I will certainly go mad.

I had not quite got the cross right for the first picture. There was something about how far apart the lines of grain should be in a large piece of wood that bothered me, and so I went down to the arsenal to look again at the ships, thinking that the sight of a large mast or beam would set me on the right track.

And there on the tract of empty land in front of the factory were the same band of children, just out of their school, all running and shouting and hopping about in that funny, frog-like fashion that children do. I became absorbed by them, for I have not often used children in my pictures, and like as not might need to at some point. Babies are one thing, but children seem to be a law unto themselves.

After a few moments, I do swear that I was beginning to feel a little more like myself. My spirits were not quite so gloomy as before. It was the sketching, I am sure of it. There is no better cure for distemper than being absorbed. I carried on sketching, keeping myself back in the shadow of a wall, for I did not want the children to become self-conscious and start posing or acting up especially for me. They are all born actors and will do that, I have noticed.

And then I saw their schoolteacher running toward me, a funny looking fellow, with copious hair flowing out of his nostrils, his gown all covered in chalk dust, and waving a heavy-looking tome in his left hand. He demanded to know what I was doing hanging around here, looking at his class. I must admit I was caught off guard, and was about to show him my sketches and explain and apologize, and then I remembered my true self, and what I was supposed to be like. Not just that either. I woke up to the implications of what he was saying, and that got me going into a rage. Under age children are not to my taste, nor to any man I know of who is worthy of the name.

Oh, I have seen men slinking off to child brothels. And sad figures they are.

And I resent the implication that this old pedant is

throwing in my face. So I drew out my dagger and waved it at him, which pulled him up short very smartly, and he started gobbling like a turkey, and I turned my hand very carefully so that the blade faced away from the good teacher and smacked him firmly across the head with the pommel of the handle which stuck out below my fist. And again for good measure on his forehead. Just enough to break his skin a little and give him a bruise, not enough to knock him over.

That shut him up good and proper and he ran off clutching his head and saying loudly that this was not the last I had heard of this, that he was connected to some duke or other, and he would have satisfaction.

I am beginning to think my life works in regular cycles, almost like a woman's. Some time goes by, and then the urge to violence comes on me. Then I have to run. More time goes by and then the same old urge. Oh dear God, what is it about me?

Our People, Our Thing

Honour! Tut, a breath,
There's no such thing in nature; a mere term
Invented to awe fools.

Ben Jonson. *Volpone*

So I set off for Palermo, which seemed as good a place as any as the next port of call, although I was wrong on that count as I later discovered. A man needs a protector. So before I left I went one last time to bid farewell to de' Lazzari, for he had been a good patron, but also because I was heedful of his advice the last time we spoke. I told him some of my troubles, but mainly I complained to him about the fact that I was being followed, and I let him think that these followers were perhaps agents of the Spanish Inquisition. No need to give too much away.

His face darkened and he became very serious at that. He asked me to leave for a short time and come back later when he had had time to think upon my problem and talk to a few people, and so I went for a siesta and returned in the early evening. He was all smiles, but there was an air about him that suggested he had set up some conspiracy to his satisfaction.

He gave me the location of a good inn in Palermo, which overlooked the harbour, yet was very quiet, for it had its own garden of palm trees around it. Dukes and princes had stayed there, but they would take me in most carefully, he explained, for he gave me a letter of introduction to the manager, a most capable man and friend of his. No payment would be required for a week or so, although I might like to do some little sketches of the man and his family, which would flatter and please him too, for he was a man of some taste, and not very fond of the Church.

Above all, said de' Lazzari, always be very courteous and very proper with him and show him much respect, perhaps rather more than you truly feel. For that is the way it is with our people, he said, stressing the 'our'. Not here in Messina perhaps, for we do not stand too much on ceremony, but there in Palermo, well, Palermo is the capital and they like a little formality.

Above all, said my merchant friend, he is an honourable man. He will always do any favour for the right man. And he will not expect it returned in the near future, or perhaps even not at all. But if he does need your help, whatsoever it be, then you are honour-bound to help him as he once helped you.

An entirely sensible arrangement, I said. Would that all men conducted themselves along such lines. The world would run more smoothly. Quite so, said de' Lazzari, quite so. And men must also realize that the law is rigid and unbending and so it must be for that is its very nature. But sometimes, just sometimes, justice is not served by the law, and a man must stand by his code of honour.

Duelling, you mean? I asked. Well, yes that is one aspect of it, and a very noble one, he said. But no, that is not quite what I was getting at, sometimes there are other matters. When the authorities become too oppressive in matters that really should be private, for example, or when a greedy landlord is starving his tenants, or when the police are unfairly framing a man for a crime he did not commit. Such matters, he said, are best dealt with among ourselves, among our friends, among men with the power to cure these . . . er . . . imbalances. For such they are, no more than a slight imbalance in the scales of justice, which can be righted by weighing in just the right amount on the unbalanced side of the scales. And such a weighing-in must be done sensibly, by men of honour, men of supreme discretion, men of silence. Like the Rosicrucians, I said, rather wildly. He smiled. I have heard speak of the Fellowship of the Rosy Cross, he said, and yes, quite like them. But here in Sicily we have our own way of doing things. He nodded and spread his hands wide and shook them up and down. It is a very Sicilian gesture. I like it.

And then he checked the shutters were closed, and locked his door properly with a very conspiratorial air and a slightly amused shrug, to suggest that it was tiresome, but sometimes these precautions are necessary. And he told me to stay within the confines of the hotel for the first week, but confide my troubles about being followed with the manager. His staff would ascertain if anyone were still following me. That is all the manager would do for me, just give me the information. After that, I will deal with it myself? I asked.

No, no that will not do at all. Palermo is not like here at all, the police will be down on your neck in no time, and you'll be hauled before some dreadful judge. No, no, listen to me carefully, he said.

Leave Palermo, by the southern gate, and avoid at all costs walking beside the shore line near the harbour, for that is one large gypsy encampment and anything could go awry if you stray among them. But leave directly and with clear intent, and look neither to your left or right, nor behind you. Do not look to see if you are followed, and do not move too quick or too slow. Do not carry much, just set out as if you were going on a single day's journey, he said.

And by late afternoon, you will reach the hilltop town of Prizzi. It is hard to find, and you must ask directions. Do not ask ostentatiously, just matter-of-factly. Do not worry, for no one will ask your intentions or why you are going there. The local peasants mind their own business and don't say very much. The path up to it is steep, so rest at the foot, and eat and drink a little, though not too much.

And when you reach the top, you will find a pleasant

little square, with a well in the middle. Go to the *osteria*, not the one nearest to the well, but the other one. Sit in there and order a meal. And tell the waiter that someone will be joining you later. Make sure that the waiter sees this ring which I give you now. It is small and it is discreet, but there is no need to flash it in his eyes. Just make sure your hand rests upon the table top, he will see it. And someone will indeed join you later. Do not make like you are old friends, don't clap him on the back and so on. Pretend that you know him only a little, and that you are there to do a little business. Some trading perhaps. Above all look serious, and treat him with great respect.

I know this man, and I know the men on that hilltop. I will try to get advance word to them, but that is not always possible. Provided you have this ring, they will listen to your problems and keep them secret. Whether they will help you or give you advice is another matter. All that is certain is that they will not harm you.

But do not worry, they will certainly tell you of their intentions. And if these people cannot rid you of your pursuers, then I doubt anyone can. In which case take the matter into your own hands, and God protect you thereafter. For if it is the Spanish Inquisition that are following you, then they will never rest, no matter how many you deal with at dead of night. Your best bet then would be to head back to Rome. I know your little difficulty there, but at least it is outside the Spanish jurisdiction. Lobby the Pope for a pardon through your friend the Cardinal. All things are possible from the Pope, for he will bend any which way if it suits his politics.

Here is the ring, see it fits fine. And remember: honour, respect, common nobility.

The Parting of Our Ways

When you go around, look and consider where men gather and how they act when they speak, and when they argue or laugh or fight together.

Leonardo da Vinci. *The Book of Painting*

Minitti and I both went to the harbour and got separate boats, he back to Syracuse, me to Palermo, the capital city of the island, about which I know nothing more than what my merchant friend has told me. As we bid farewell, Minitti was suddenly overcome, and like as not to start weeping. This was not like him. I told him I would return and we would see each other again, but there was more to it than that. I could see he was very upset about something, and gulping all the time, and walking away, then returning toward me with his head hung.

I got the distinct feeling that he wanted to confess something to me. But I am not good at this sort of thing. Finally, just as his boat was leaving, he said in a choking voice that the Spanish Inquisition had come to him and questioned him about a matter of bigamy, which he had not fully sorted

239

out in his life, him having married some woman in Rome, before taking his current wife in Syracuse.

'And did it come out all right?' I asked.

'Of course it did,' he said miserably, 'for here I am, unharmed, at liberty, talking to you . . .' and with that he had to run on board his ship which was just about to cast off the gangplank. I called out '*Addio*,' and I watched him go until he was lost to view. Neither of us waved. And I turned about and retraced my steps to my tavern to think upon our parting and what he had said. I never made it back.

The full import came to me suddenly, and I had to sit for a while, at first on the wall of a fountain, and later in an inn, for I needed a stiff drink or two.

It was Minitti who betrayed me. Why else had he come to Messina except to point me out to those who were tracking me? He must have done a deal with the Inquisition. But why would the Spanish Inquisition want to track me down, it makes no sense. True, I have lived on Spanish territory, indeed I am in it now. But I have never offended that race, not its priests. Perhaps they have some connection with Alof in Malta, for there is certainly a Spanish chapter of the knights quartered there. And perhaps he persuaded them to hunt me down here, because a Spanish contingent would have better luck, here in Spanish territory. But that makes no sense either.

Alof would want as few people as possible knowing about his sins. He would just dispatch one of those five knights who arrested me, and they would follow me about the island with impunity. Indeed that is who I thought the veiled figure that Minitti frightened must have been. No, surely, these strange people following me must be *assassini* of the Knights of Malta, not the Spanish.

But Minitti just all but confessed before he left that he had fingered me to the Spanish lot. If so, it must be that they have teamed up with their opposite numbers in the Vatican. I've crossed them badly enough in the past, God knows, with my blasphemy and my spying and then killing the Papist Ranuccio. Now they want me under wraps. All of them, Spanish, Vatican, maybe they've even teamed up with the Maltese too, just for good measure

Oh shit. Exit artist, pursued by thirty thousand screaming furies. Still, the thought perked me up from under my illness a little. Nothing like the prospect of being horribly buggered up to get a man going.

Poor Minitti. What must it be like to be so frightened that you will betray a friend? As frightened as I am feeling now? Mmmm, no, no, not that far yet, I am not so far gone I would sell my mate.

So Palermo was suddenly recommending itself to me with some urgency. A new and strange place in which I would be unknown and maybe could shake off my predators, perhaps with Lazzari's cunning plan.

The journey was short, less than two days' sailing, and I sneaked a look at as many of my fellow passengers as I could.

But I could see nothing suspicious. But then I wouldn't. I am not good at this clandestine thing. I wish I had paid more heed to Vialardi's little lectures on the subject. I wish Vialardi were here in fact. I never liked the man much, but if ever a mortal man was in need of his skills it is I.

There was an archbishop in Palermo who wanted my services. I won't bore you with the details, but he was related to a family, the Colonnas, I had done some work for in the past – indeed, who had protected me after the fracas in Rome. Word of me gets around here. He wanted another Nativity.

So I did one a bit different from the plain one in Messina. And I have to admit, I put in a large amount of the crappy sort of religious detail that he wanted. I am too tired, too old, too defeated to argue any more. You want a few yards of swirling drapery? You may have it. You want adoring angels fluttering above the whole thing? Why certainly. You want St Francis and St Lawrence present at the birth, even though they weren't born at the time, or were a thousand miles away? No problem, I will put them here and there, as they would have been in spirit, just so.

I give in. No more fighting. No more arguing, you win. I will be a good boy and do as I am told. Until I feel better anyway, then just watch me. Joseph I decided not to turn into an old dotard this time around and painted him from the rear as a young man with a mop of blond hair. Poor pageboy, I wonder what became of you. Still with Alof I expect, though under much suspicion. Or maybe not, if he had acted under Alof's orders. How can I know? It may be he who is at the root of all this, but I am still fond of his memory.

The baby Jesus I couldn't be bothered with, just left him lying on the ground ignored, as if he had been chucked away as not sufficiently interesting.

No one noticed.

And all the while I stayed at the inn by the harbour, surrounded by the palm trees, as recommended by de' Lazzari, and it was all just as he said. The manager was very proud, very grave and altogether to be taken seriously. I sketched his wife and sons and daughters one morning while he supervised the kitchens and he was most pleased. I will do him soon, when he has a free hour, and then, while we are alone, I will tell him of my troubles. For while I saw no one on the voyage, yet I am still watched, I know it. The feeling is inescapable, oppressive, very troubling. I cannot sleep again, and I start awake five or six times in the middle of the night, sometimes from a sound, sometimes from some other thing which I then cannot discover. I constantly check over my shoulder and am much given to using reflections to see what lies behind my back. It is very wearing. A tic has developed in the corner of my right eye and twitches constantly, and gives me an even more shifty look. Still, that's no bad thing. I notice the other people at the inn don't talk to me. For which much thanks.

I painted the manager one afternoon, during the siesta hour, for he was very busy and he broached the subject of my troubles even before I raised the matter. He talked of de' Lazzari and what a good and honourable friend he was. And then he smiled almost imperceptibly and spoke softly yet very distinctly. Did I know I was being followed? Well, yes, but I did not know who by, or where or when.

'Almost constantly,' he said, 'and it is impossible to say by how many, for they change and change about, and all seem to have been chosen for their similar build and colouring, and they frequently wear the Arab veil and turban, which is not at all uncommon around here, as you will have seen. This place has been Moorish in its time.'

'I do not know what to do,' I admitted wretchedly, 'I am in your hands.'

'No,' he said, 'I think not, looking at you and knowing your reputation. You are a strong man, a man of *virtù*. But you must banish from your mind these fears that do so overwhelm you. These men may be agents from some large power, but they are not phantoms, or ghosts, or wizards. Nor yet saints nor prophets nor miracle workers. They are merely mortal, and any mortal man may be dealt with, according to his deserts.'

And just his saying that greatly lifted my spirits, for of course he is right. There is nothing dangerous that the mind will not make more so by brooding.

'Permit me to help a little if I may,' he said. 'I am not a powerful man, but I know men around here, it is part of my trade, you understand, men who are clever, men who can, how can I put this . . . do things. At least, in this case, I think we must first find some things out. Knowledge is power, my friend, an old saying and one of the many true things my father taught me. Permit me, please, it would do me a great honour to help a friend of my good friend de' Lazzari.'

'It is I who would be honoured,' I said. And he bowed low.

'It is a very good likeness,' he said as he looked at my oil sketch, 'but perhaps too kind to me.' I bowed, and assured him not. 'So, so,' he said, 'I will see you again soon.' 'À bientôt,' I said. I'm glad he is inside my tent, and not outside. I would not trust him an inch.

Sure enough he came to me in my room the next day early and spoke again softly but distinctly. I noticed that he never faltered when he spoke, but said his words rather as if he had been an actor and learnt his lines already by heart. Though without any actor's inflections or emphases. His tone was a very even one, and so, while his meaning was always clear, it was often hard to guess any hidden or secondary meaning that he might have been implying. It was also impossible to guess what he was feeling. No doubt that was the idea.

'There are no more than five of them, and they are staying in a palazzo here owned by a Spanish count, although the count is currently back in Spain and has been so for some year and a half. So it is hard to tell if they are under his orders or some others to whom the count is paying a favour or is answerable to. Whether they themselves are Spanish is also moot. Certainly they go about veiled, although they frequently talk to men who are not. Yet the unveiled men do not seem to be shadowing you. It is only the veiled ones, and they number no more than five. They are expert. They can even follow you by staying ahead of you in the street so that you can only see their back. If they then lose you, well there is always a back-up man some distance behind, and they chop and change. You will not shake them off at all easily.'

I suddenly inhaled very sharply, and my breath caught at the back of my throat, as if a cricket had jumped into my mouth, and got jammed there. I realized that I had forgotten to breathe for the last few minutes, and now I was trying to fill my lungs at twice the normal sort of rate, but had lost the knack of how to do it. 'How do people breathe?' I remember thinking, 'How does it work?' And the world was washed with dark crimson. The manager sat me down and patted my shoulder until the odd colour drained from my eyes and the room looked brown again. The sawing noise from the back of my throat quieted and I could once more breathe a little, though there was still a stoppage in my throat, as if a small wooden gate had been closed in there, and the air could only get past it in small eddies. And finally I thought that I might still live, in spite of it all.

There is a Green Hill Far Away

Assassiner c'est le plus court chemin
– Assassination is the quickest way

Molière (Jean-Baptiste Poquelin). Le Sicilien (1668)

'What I suggest is this,' the manager continued, 'that you go out of town to the place that de' Lazzari told you about. It is my guess that once you are seen leaving this town, then only one or two will follow you out into the countryside. The others will regroup to report to their leader, perhaps await your return and consider what next to do. The waiter in the *osteria* on the hilltop town will have a solution to your problem.'

I set out early the next morning, with a satchel containing a little bread and water, but no more. That should make it plain enough to them that I would be gone but a day or two. The countryside was parched dry, the dust, the earth, the few scant trees were all a pale yellow-green, and the sun was pitiless. God I hate the country.

And by mid-afternoon I was in Prizzi, although the name did not appear on any signpost or milestone and I often had to ask the way. The locals around here are very shifty and do not look at you when they reply and often cross themselves though not very convincingly, as if they might be making a show for a priest. They all act as if they know something important, which I don't know. Yet none deceived me in the directions they gave, and none tried to rob me. A strange place.

And sure enough, there was the square, perched high on the hill, with much greenery and soft hanging plants on the walls, which was nice, and a fine view of the surrounding country through the gaps and alleys of the houses. There were figs and olives in abundance, hanging from the many trees. And there was the *osteria*. Just as I had been told. And in I went. And instantly the place went silent and they all turned to look at me. I stared back and they stared back and then they returned their gaze to whatever they were doing before, like looking at their porridge, except for one villainous *paisano*, who kept a swivel eye upon me all the time I was there. I found a table in the corner and sat down and stretched my back and neck for I was stiff from the journey.

A waiter appeared and put a carafe of wine on the table. I said I had not ordered wine, and he shrugged and said it was all there was, unless I wanted water, in which case there was a well outside. Well, damn that sort of attitude. I jumped up and very nearly did to him what I told you I did in Rome to a cheeky waiter, but then I remembered where

I was and what de' Lazzari had told me. And recovered myself very quick and sat down. And placed my left hand on the table, where he could see the ring, which Lazzari had given me. It was impossible to say whether he noticed it, but I drank some of the wine and it was very, very good, a pink colour not at all like the deep red of the mainland, and slightly flavoured with fennel of all things, but very refreshing and strangely clarifying to the mind. Or perhaps that was the mountain air.

And presently the waiter bought me food, without my having ordered either, so I guess he had seen the ring, or maybe that is just the way things are around here. There was a dish of some sardine mush, with raisins and peppers and almonds mixed in, and then a dish of quails drenched in a sauce of *funghi*, again with fennel, and some local cheese with seeds in it. And some pastry with honey and more almonds and a drink made from ewe's milk and more wine. They eat well here on this island.

As the pastry dish arrived, a man entered carrying a fearsome wheel lock, the flint of which he carefully unlocked and lowered to its pan, and leant the gun in a corner near to my table. He came and sat next to me, as if it had all been arranged beforehand, although he was not over-familiar, just a curt nod and greeting before he sat at my right hand. The waiter bought him some food too, although it was much simpler than mine and I could not see what it was. It reeked of garlic, though, and hot peppers. He tucked into it with some relish, although his manners were better than you might expect, for although he was not a peasant, yet his hands were quite rough, and his skin well tanned by the sun.

He wore a short sleeveless jacket of dark thick woollen material, worn smooth by use, and covered in pockets down its front, for fishing tackle or for ball and powder I would guess. And a strange hat, again of dark wool, but pulled forward to form a peak over the eyes. Useful I would guess for the sun, for there is little shade outside the town.

And in between spoonfuls of food, he had a habit of looking at you, yet not quite looking at you. I got the impression that without moving the balls in their sockets, his eyes could take in everything that there was to see, whether in this room, or out in the country. His eyes were a pale grey and very steady. So was his hand, which did not shake at all. Altogether he was a very steady man, not given to sudden or unnecessary movement.

'Were the quails good?' he enquired, although he had not seen me eat them. 'Very good,' I said. 'Good,' he said, 'I shot them this morning.' 'With that?' I asked, pointing at the wheel lock. 'No,' he said, 'that is too heavy for a quail. It would destroy the whole bird . . . No, for quail you use a light gun . . . with lead shot which scatters . . . so that only a small pellet will enter the bird . . . enough to kill it . . . but not spoil the meat.' He spoke in brief phrases as if conserving his words as precious.

I was about to ask him what he hunted with the wheel

lock, but then thought better of it. It was a big gun, often needing a rest to support it, and I had seen the Pope's escort once use one in Rome on a man who was threatening them, and the explosion and the bullet damn near severed his trunk in two. A messy business and one I did not wish to enquire further about.

'And this bird gun, where is that?' I asked, just by way of conversation.

'My "Lupo",' he said, 'it is round the back . . . where I can get at it if I need . . . It has only a short barrel . . . for I have sawn a length off . . . it is easily carried.'

' "Lupo"?' I said. 'Why do you call it that?'

'Have you ever looked into a wolf's throat?' he said.

I nodded to suggest I understood, and swallowed heavily. I had indeed once been attacked by a wolf, when I was wandering about Lombardy on my way to Rome. It was darkening, and I do not know why he was not in a pack, for they usually do not bother men unless they are very hungry and in a pack. But he came at me even as I was building a fire for the night, perhaps he aimed to get me before I had a good fire going, but I lifted a flaming brand in my left hand which gave him pause, and with my sword in my right I thrust at his muzzle and nose. Caught him squarely too, straight down the back of his gizzard, but just before my sword found its mark, I looked clear down his throat. It was black as the hinges of hell.

I knew what this man meant all right.

We finished our meal, and he sat back and stretched slightly, his breath reeking of garlic, which I do not mind at all.

I looked down at my dish for a while, collecting my thoughts and my self and how best I might approach my topic, and then I opened my mouth to speak, and he raised his hand, gently, not unkindly, but unmistakably to silence me.

'It will be taken care of,' he said, and looked slowly around the inn, as if he were looking into the middle distance.

'They may be powerful . . .' I began, but he raised his hand again and shrugged.

'How may I pay you?' I said, and he looked mildly offended, though only very briefly, before his face assumed its mask-like calm.

'It will all be taken care of,' he said again.

'When you have taken care of it, I would like to know, not who they were, but who had sent them. Where they were from, so to speak?' I said.

He spoke without looking at me. 'Two are from Malta,' he said, 'and two are from Rome.' He paused and then said, 'One from Rome and one from Malta stayed in Palermo. One from Rome and one from Malta followed you here. Does that tell you enough?'

'Are they here, in this town? Why did I not see them?'

'They are good trackers,' he said, and smiled. 'Perhaps

they learned their skills here in Sicily, from one of ours. Or perhaps from the Berbers of Libya, for they too are expert at following men unseen even in the desert where there is no cover. And they wear the veil, which is their trademark. It does not matter much. Where they are, you need not know. You may stay the night and return tomorrow and you will be quite safe while out here. In Palermo, I cannot guarantee. But the odds will be much better for you. Only two left and they will be frightened by the news of their friends. And the hotel manager will help, again.'

He turned his grey eyes on me again, and suddenly all the questions I wanted to ask vanished from my mind, like dark shadows on a wall, which dissolve in the sunlight when a window is thrown open. 'Do not worry,' he said, 'it will all be taken care of.'

The next day I set out at dawn. No one bid me farewell, and I descended from the hill town with some relief, and set out across the scrubby farms and olive groves toward Palermo again. Though this time my heart was lighter. I even hummed a tune. Until I heard two sudden sharp noises, like the crack of a thick tree branch breaking, but each with a long withdrawing echo as it resounded through the hills. My new friend, out hunting quail again, no doubt.

And after a half-hour or so, I turned about to look back once more at Prizzi, high on its hill, and I could see a small flock of birds just outside the city, but near the main road that I had traversed. I am not good at recognizing birds. But these were very large and they glided slowly rather than flapping their wings. I think I know which birds those are. And they were circling.

I hummed a little song I had not heard since I was in Rome at a tennis match when some spectators were chanting it to a popular tune. 'All Papists are bastards.' I liked it, for it got some dark looks from people dotted around in the crowd, so you could pick out the pro-Papists quite quickly. Out here, though, it got a bit lost in the wind and the wide open spaces, and I felt a bit foolish, so I shut up and carried on back to Palermo and who knows what?

I would happily have done for them myself, but how could I, when, for the life of me, I couldn't find them?

I don't like guns, nasty noisy things, and cowardly too. When I kill a man, I look in his face.

I arrived back at my hotel opposite the harbour with the palms all about it, making it shady in the late afternoon, and the doorman took me aside and ushered me into the manager's office, and closed the door, without looking inside himself. As I stood in the office I could see why he had been loath to enter. There on the manager's table were two turbans of dark material, with a swathe of veil uncoiled around them. They both sat there on the table like wigs on a wig-maker's block. What was inside them, making them keep their shape and stay upright, I did not care to ask. Nor how they came to be there before I had even returned.

The manager sat behind his table, contemplating the two things before him. 'Hmm,' he said with some satisfaction after a moment, 'round one to us, I think. I will use these to good effect.'

I snorted a brief laugh at this, which caused him to smile, the first I had seen him do. 'How?' I said.

'We must make sure that the two who remained here in Palermo are, ah, apprised of their comrades' fate,' he said. 'By this evening, I will deliver . . . these . . .' he waved a languid hand over the turbans, 'to their prospective owners. What they do then will be interesting.'

'Interesting to you, no doubt,' I said, 'probably fatal to me.'

'This could well prove true, my friend,' he said, 'I have thought this through quite carefully, and it seems to me that I must do what I must, and they in turn will pursue one of two possible courses. Either they will be dismayed, and will *reculer pour mieux sauter*, so to speak. In plain language they will run home with their tails up their arses and whine to their masters and plot another plan. Or, they will be made of sterner stuff, and get whipped up into an absolute frenzy over what we have done, and come after you with renewed vigour. I hope for the first, I fear for the second. My friend,' he said, and again he bowed slightly, even though still sitting, 'I think that Palermo is no longer a temperate place for you.'

I looked at the turbans again. Something black and sticky was seeping out from under one. And I could not but agree.

I wondered where I could go next, and the manager read my thoughts. 'Rome of course would finally be the best place. You are known there, you have protectors, you still have the reputation as their best painter, and the Spanish may have some influence, but no jurisdiction. That leaves the Vatican, or rather their secret service, which in turn means the Jesuits, who are still after your skin, or perhaps something else from you. But they can be contained. If only you can get a pardon from the Pope for that wretched murder of Ranuccio. It really was not a clever thing to do at the time.'

He was extraordinary. He spoke all the above at an even pace without inflection, yet he knew exactly my circumstances and exactly what was open to me. How he came by all this intelligence I do not know, although I suspect de' Lazzari at least as the immediate person behind it all. And after de' Lazzari, who knows who up the chain of command . . .

He was right, though. Rome was my best hope. How then to get around the Pope's price upon my head?

Again the manager read my mind.

'The Cardinal del Monte is still your best bet,' he said. 'He loved you much once, and he loves you still even though you have not heard from him all the while. His influence is less than it once was, for his allies are out of favour with the Pope's circle at the moment. But still he has some clout. And he is still young and healthy. In these matters, the wheel of fate often turns full circle, and a man's hour may come around again a second time. I would not be surprised if one day he succeeded to the highest office. But in the meantime, he remains your best hope of extracting a pardon from the current Pope.'

He paused slightly and formed his fingers into a steeple. That is often a sign of a man lying, I have found, as if he seeks to hide inside the edifice he has built of his fingers. But not here and now I think. The manager was just generally weighing things up before his summation.

'He will be in Naples from tomorrow,' he said.

'And so will I,' I thought, but did not say. 'And how in hell do you know all this stuff?' I also thought.

I bowed low this time, and voiced my eternal gratitude in words that even I began to half-believe. For indeed I was most grateful, although I could do without all this stuff with the turbans. It looks like a game of crazy vendetta to me. Still, he has done me much service, and I must take pains at least to acknowledge it, for there is little I can do by way of repayment at present.

He waved aside my thanks with the usual local hand gesture and then asked me most politely if I would deliver a small package for him to a friend in Naples. I found myself almost begging to be allowed to help him out with this small chore. Only later did I realize that almost everything he said was as if my whole future were mapped out and preordained. And by him to boot.

Very strange, but of course I said yes, and took a packet from him and there and then set out straight away for the harbour. No need to return to my room. I had my sword and my dagger and my money about me. What else does a man need?

And I caught the second to last boat of the season, for the storms were building up lately and voyages will soon be severely curtailed. Which is good for me, and bad for my followers.

More sea.

More vomit.

Neapolitan Nightmare

Much drinking, little thinking.

Swift. *Journal to Stella. 1768*

Back in Naples, and still I did not like the place. It teems with life, far too much of it for its own good, crowded, noisy, smelly.

I found my way back to my old digs, which were still there, and put on a clean shirt, the first in weeks, and went out to celebrate a little on my own. I managed to get back to my rooms even though I was very drunk, and slept heavily. And I dreamed of Fillide yet again, as I always seem to these days. I woke in the early hours sweating and could not return to sleep so continued drinking until I fell down dead drunk at seven in the morning. This is getting beyond a joke. I staggered around the next day, feeling as though I had been poisoned. At least I feel nothing by way of emotion. Drink is good at that; kills it stone dead. Drank some more and felt better still. Will have to stop soon. Do more work.

The drinking jag lasted a week, after which I woke one

morning in some strange tart's bed with no memory of how I had got there, or what I had been doing for six days. I went downstairs, and out into the alley until I found a café, and there drank about a gallon of water and had some coffee and tobacco. The shakes started up again very badly and I had to steady my hand by binding a scarf about it. And I had a grappa, just the one, to steady my nerves, which did the trick, and I returned to my quarters and slept.

Caught sight of myself in the glass. I am yellow as a Spanish canary cage bird. Ho, the irony.

Up early the next day, and quite sober again, and harbouring dark thoughts about my future.

I must seek out del Monte, but am not sure where to start.

I found my old patroness, the Marchesa da Caravaggio (no relation, she's just from the same town as me, that's all), who I don't think I have mentioned before, but she has a lovely place, the Palazzo Chiaia, which has a garden green with orange trees, one of my most favourite colour combinations in nature, although I have not used it in a painting for many a long year. Anyway, she put me up, the old dear. She is fifty-five and a right battleaxe, but she has been a faithful sweetie to me over the years and loves it when I turn up on her doorstep with a bloody nose and a hangdog look. She was born to take men in and look after them.

She told me that del Monte is staying at the Viceroy Benevente's place with his friend Cardinal Montalto, seeking to find out the Spanish court's intentions, and build a few bridges there for the Pope. It says much for del Monte's agreeable nature that the Spanish take him in quite happily and talk to him, in spite of his well-known affiliation to the French faction in his earlier years. Ah, what it is to be a diplomat.

I was granted an entry to Benevente's and left my card and we duly met the next day. He greeted me like a long-lost friend, and indeed that is what were to each other, though I have not seen him these four years now since I have been on the run. And he asked after my adventures most kindly, and I told him an abbreviated version, and left out the fact that I had been followed. And quite possibly still was, I had to remind myself.

He explained about the Pope, and how he did not have quite so much influence there as before, but that the usual time for a pardon to be granted for a murder, if the man be in exile, was exactly four years, which must be approaching fast. And he would use a young new cardinal, Gonzaga, to approach the Pope. For Gonzaga was a coming man, only twenty-three years old, but keen on art, and most desirous of having a genuine Caravaggio in his collection.

'He may have a dozen, free of charge, if he gain me a pardon,' I said.

Del Monte smiled and said: 'Do not price yourself too cheaply, my dear. You will need money back in Rome, the price of bread is gone through the roof, and the cost of living has risen something terrible.'

We parted for he had to go to a banquet which Benevente was throwing for some foreign dignitaries that evening.

And I called again a few days later, and he had fallen terribly ill, according to his servants. He was in his bed and close to death and poisoning was suspected for he had been in good fettle in spite of his age. Doctors were called from as far afield as Florence and they did their usual thing of taking their fees and saying there was nothing to be done, nature would take its course, and here is some expensive medicine which will purge him. And so Benevente ordered round the clock prayers, and I very nearly joined in so worried was I. If del Monte goes, then I will be left not quite high and dry, but one patron less.

He did eventually recover, but while he lay abed, my mind began to seethe. For what had put poor del Monte at death's door in the first place? If poison, then who administered it? I had been seen consorting with him quite openly. Can it be my enemies who have got to him? Why would they wish to hurt him? As a message to me. And as a message to others, which says: have nothing to do with the painter man. He is an outcast, and he is a marked man.

That sounds about right. My followers must have been closer upon my heels than I thought. Perhaps they got the last boat out of Palermo. Perhaps they have other agents here on the mainland. And now they have poisoned del

Monte. It can only be those bastards the Jesuits within the Inquisition. They always hated my paintings. And they always hated del Monte for standing by me, and for sticking up for the French faction. They support their Spanish brethren because of the Inquisition connection. And the knights of Malta? They may well be in all this stew, somewhere in the background, pulling strings, sending messages, launching off their armed thugs in my direction. Alof must have been trading intelligence with the Pope, about me, about del Monte. Christ, what a right bugger's muddle.

He is running scared over the queer thing with his pageboy, and maybe he wants me out of the way, and maybe he needs to stay well in with the Pope and all his intentions about the French, indeed about everything.

It is beginning to make sense.

Get a gun or two

Fight the good fight with all thy might.

John Samuel Monsell. Hymn. 1863

Once again I feel the hot breath of the wolf, warming the back of my collar. I wish I had my Sicilian friends about me again. I wish I had that walloping great wheel lock, primed, loaded and cocked. That would equalize the odds a little. I must get one.

So I went to an armourer, a Swede with a workshop halfway up the hill from Benevente's palazzo, and hefted one in my hands. Christ it was heavy. Hardly your handy weapon of choice to tote around the taverns of an evening. You'd look like a soldier returning from the wars with that over your shoulder. You could start a siege.

'No, no,' said the Swede, in that funny accent they have, 'what you need, I am thinking, is a handgun. Look at what I have here on this bench.' He had that straw hair, which is common among people of the north. They drink a lot too, and I like them for it. He showed me an Arab *miquelet*, a long pistol with elaborate engravings on the butt and face-plates, which were lovely. It had a large round pommel at the base of the stock, for resting on the thigh if on horseback. Its barrel was on the long side, but that made it more accurate and it looked like a very good frightener. Pull one of those out, and your enemy gets the shits in very short order. And it fitted in my belt nicely.

It needed some work done on the lock and pan, so I put down some money as a deposit, and promised the Swede I would return in a day or so.

Too late.

That evening I went down the via Sanfelice toward the port and stopped at the Osteria del Cerriglio, the place run by that German with the great sense of humour. It's a lovely, lovely place. Two very nice big rooms, good food, nicely decorated with dirty pictures in the corners of people going at it, and if that raises your fancy then you have one of the women in the upstairs rooms. They are resident whores. Now I ask you, what more could a *valent'uomo* want of an evening? That Spanish author wrote some of *Don Quixote* there I believe, so the place is inspirational too. The local poet Basile had described it in some good food guide as being the sort of place 'which makes you live to be a hundred'. Not me it didn't.

It nearly did for me.

I went in via the courtyard at the back with the lovely trelliswork and the fountain splashing in the background, and I was barely in the garden gate before they set on me, and I had no chance to draw my sword. God knows where all the diners were, no doubt this bunch of assassins had cleared them out, or done a deal with the landlord.

One man, I could not see him for he was hid behind the door into the garden, seized me from behind around the waist, trapping both my arms, or so he thought. Another lunged straight at me with his sword. I am not heavy, so I knew I could not unbalance the man behind me, who had me lifted partly from the ground. So I stamped my heel down hard upon the top of his foot, just back from the toes, and I felt the bones crunch beneath my heel, and he screamed and crumpled slightly. I sank with him. And took the sword full in the face.

It hit me hard upon the cheek and sliced straight through and jammed into my teeth. And I felt a couple go from their sockets, but thank God for my strong teeth, the blade was stopped there, by my upper jaw I think. I could feel the blade bend, and spring against the jaw bone. And it hurt like hell. But better through the cheek than through the lung. I let out a roar, and the man drew back, taking his sword with him. And there were two others standing round with him, not to mention the man behind me who had seized me and was slackening his grip fast, no doubt because he wanted to rub his injured foot.

And do you know? They thought it was all over.

Stupid apes.

I ran the man behind me through with my dagger in one

neat move, stabbing him upwards from under his ribcage, then up through the stomach and into a lung. I didn't even turn around to do it, just swung backwards at where I could feel that he was. He inhaled loudly and fell. Then I set to the man who had stabbed my cheek. He was back on his guard, quite quick, and I had only my dagger, so I closed with him, and felt his sword between my arm and my ribs. He was sawing away with it, and I felt it bite against my ribs, but that was all right, I can live with that, for the point cannot enter me, and he could not disengage. And I did the same thing with my dagger, held upwards; in at the belly, the soft part, then push upward under the ribs. He departed this life quite quick too.

Then a stool crashed onto my head, thanks to one of the others, although his aim was not good, and my neck and shoulder took the brunt, so it did not knock me out. I fell to my knees, and shook my head, quite groggy now, and I could feel a large flap of skin from my cut cheek flopping against my jaw, like a wet rag. That was going to hurt like hell later. Right now, though, the hurt can wait. Staying alive is my main idea. They started kicking. One aimed a real beauty at my temple, which could have been the end of me, but hit the top of my head and did nothing.

From where I was down on the ground, I found my dagger again, and reversed it in my hand, with one neat flip (I told you I learnt my stuff well from the armourer). I saw my chance and slashed out in one sweeping arc, which ended neatly on the Achilles' tendon of one them. That will leave him lame for life. He started squealing like a trapped wild pig too. Three down, where was that fourth?

I never found him. The next I knew was a blow to the back of the head and the back, then more and more; and then one of the upstairs windows opened, and as if from a great distance, I could hear one of the women hanging out the window and screaming blue murder. *Assassino, assassino.*

God bless that whore. I owe my life to her.

They fled, and I was falling through a black hole that opened up beneath me. And just before I went under, I felt that lurch to the stomach, and a feeling of triumph, and a strong desire to smile, just for myself alone. I had not felt that since . . . Oh, since the last time I murdered a man.

Loppy face

I have heard of your paintings too well enough.
God hath given you one face and you make yourselves another

William Shakespeare, *Hamlet (1601)*

I came around later in bed at the palazzo.

I called for a glass, and found I could not speak too well, as I had rags stuffed in my mouth. They were loath to give me one, but I started to get up and so they pushed me back down on the bed and fetched a small mirror just to keep me from searching for it myself.

Jesus Christ, I looked like a *zuppa inglese* that was rotten with maggots. Someone had stitched my cheek back together with what looked like a leather bridle thong. I had no teeth along one side of my upper jaw, and several were missing from the lower. The sword had penetrated my palate too, a few more inches and it would have been into my brainpan. As it was, I would never get my taste back properly, nor could I rightly pronounce certain words, the ones that needed the tongue on the roof of the mouth, but lisped like a little girl.

My gums were raw, and bleeding still. The rest of my face was lopsided from the beating, with one eye socket crushed and making the eye all shot with blood and leery. The rest of my face was covered with bruising, a purple and yellow colour. It looked like a bad case of skin disease. Or my old malaria come back to haunt me. It is strange how it did not hurt until now. Such is the way it goes, when your blood is up, you do not notice pain. Now I did. My face smarted like the sting of death.

Ah, well, I never was a pretty boy.

I will say this in its favour, though. I doubt any future would-be assassins will be able to follow me quite so easily. Christ, my own mother wouldn't recognize me.

From now on I'll just have to depend upon a lady's pity, or maybe her liking for a rough sort of man. I have never been under any illusions about my looks anyway. Before, women would go with me for other reasons, or else I would pay. Now, well, they will just have to pity me. It'll work, I'm sure.

I wonder where Fillide is? I could do with her right now. She alone of all women could look on my ugly face without flinching. She could always see behind the surface of all things. And she could always look through my ugliness to whatever lay inside me. I do not say that what she saw there was even very nice. But she took me for what I was, and that is a great gift. I often think of her. And my thoughts these days are always kind. Such is the gift of ageing or the nearness of death.

I was told that the knights were dismayed when I fought back so hard. Two were dead or dying, one limping badly, and the fourth frightened out of his wits, and they were only content that I was inert on the floor, whether dead or no, for they were too busy retreating to lick their wounds. I learnt that the remaining two were not even armed with a sword, so sure were they of what they were doing; and to that fact, as well as to the whore, I owe my life. Although that does seem strange, if it is the knights of Malta who are after me.

Four full-blown knights, all trained fighting men, going out to do a blood job on someone, and yet two of them go unarmed? And then leave the job unfinished?

I don't believe it. Those thugs never leave their sword behind. Nor walk out on a victim who is down but not out. It must have been someone else.

Well, we all know who. I mean the choices aren't very numerous, are they? They tried to poison del Monte and make it look like food poisoning after a banquet. Then they try to murder me and make it look like a tavern brawl. Really those Vatican boys are such rank amateurs, they would bungle a drinking party at a vineyard. I really thought they were better at this sort of thing.

Obviously they can only ever get anything right if they have you alone, bound head and foot, in their torture chamber. Further reason to hate them. They are sadists and cowards to a man. God rot them all, I'll seek them out and kill them all, till the Tiber is clogged with their bodies and Vatican Square runs red with their guts, and their cellars brim full with their blood. I hate them, I hate them, I hate them more than I hate death, and I will never rest till I have killed more. And I'll follow them down to the ninth circle and keep them there, in agony, at the point of my sword, for a thousand years, and I shall not mind the flames.

Those two I just killed were for Bruno. And that's not enough. He was worth fifty of the Jesuits. He was worth the whole boiling lot of them. I spit on their worthless souls.

Sorry. I do get a bit worked up sometimes. My rage was once all that kept me going, and I am pleased when it strikes up again. It does me good, for I feel the pain receding and my blood is up in my veins, such that I want to get out of bed. So I tried that.

And they came and scraped me off the floor and put me back in bed with much fussing. The nuns here are rather sweet. I do like nuns. I often think about jumping one. Not that half of them would object, they are only younger daughters who are difficult or who have no dowry, poor cows. Perhaps I'll marry one, when I am better. There's a thought. I am reaching an age now when a man ought to be a little more settled.

What can I be thinking of? It must be the drugs they are

giving me. Something of the poppy, I like that stuff. It washes away your cares and makes life seem worth living.

Well, perhaps that is going a bit too far.

I'll never marry, I know it, nor will I know what other men take pleasure in, such as children and a settled life, it is not for me.

One of the nuns gave me a Roman news sheet of two days ago. It carries an item about my death. 'There has come from Naples the news that Caravaggio the famous painter has been killed . . .'

No obituary, though. A pity, for I would like to have read that.

I wrote to their office: 'You exaggerate the news of my death.' They didn't run an apology.

Twelve Good Pictures

Fie upon this quiet life. I want work.

Shakespeare. *Henry IV Part I. 1597*

It was nine months before I was altogether well again, what with the fevers and the infections. And during that time I rattled them out. The illness was a perfect reason to stay indoors and do my work and not go roistering. That, and the fact that a hundred thousand armed bastards paid for by the Vatican secret service were all baying for my blood.

I must have done near a dozen good works. I was getting quicker and quicker and because I was sleeping so deep with all the drugs and herbs they were giving me, so too my pictures often seemed to sleepwalk. They became dreamy and floated free like submarine creatures from the unplumbed deep. Not that I painted monsters, it is just the style I am speaking of.

For a month, though, before that, the fever was at its worst and the night sweats were unabated. I weighed no more than a cat. The nuns would feed me thin soup, but it came back up my gorge and bit on the back of my throat and tasted vile on my tongue. A kindly friar swabbed my body most lovingly every few hours, but the sheets on my bed were always sopping.

I can raise myself on one elbow, no more than that. Was it yesterday that I spoke with the Marchesa? I am not sure, for night follows day with no distinction and my memory slides one thing into another. I feel that my time may be at hand. Pick it up, pick it up.

When improved, I did another of Salome, with John's head in a basin, which I sent off to Alof, by post-haste courier service. Let him think it is a peace offering.

Actually it's not a peace offering at all, I am rubbing his nose in it. What I am saying is: I am still alive and I know what I know, in spite of what any assassins have tried. I'd like to bet that he's in touch with the Vatican too. He must be giving at the very least his assent to the attempts on my life, if not his active support. They are as keen as he to keep the status quo firmly in place, so even if they know of his sexual tastes they are not about to rock the Maltese boat. Better by far to get me out of the way, preferably in the middle of nowhere, with no witnesses.

My only hope is that someone, somewhere still wants my paintings. I am still the feted man I once was. My star has not declined, in the way that my life has. I command even higher fees than before. People still want my art on their chapel walls and in their homes. Let's hope they have the ear of the Pope as regularly as the Jesuits.

I did a *Crucifixion of St Andrew*.

I did a *Christ Arisen*.

I did a *David and Goliath*.

And I did a *St Ursula*. She was the mad one who took off into the wild with eleven thousand virgins in tow, all of whom got the chop from the Huns, serve them right for going to Germany. I remember I saw a whole cycle of paintings in Venice devoted to her life story. Carpaccio, was it? They were all rubbish.

She got killed by a Hun too, who shot an arrow in her at point-blank range. Serve her right. She had said 'No thanks' to him when he offered her his hand in marriage. Silly girl. All she had to do was say, 'Let me think about it.' It always amazes me just how stupid most of our saints and martyrs are. If they are supposed to be an example to us all, no wonder the country is in such a ruin. Farmers starving outside the city gates, *banditi* roaming the countryside unchecked, beggars everywhere inside the city, orphans, mendicants, cripples, crime rife, and people like me allowed to kill each other over a game of tennis; what is the world coming to? And what with the price of corn . . .

Ursula is looking at the arrow in her stomach with an appalled fascination.

St Andrew is on his cross preaching, and taking two long days to die.

My Risen Christ looks like a criminal caught in the act.

I am sure you can see the way my brain was turning

And David and Goliath I have done before, but this time there is a difference. David holds the head at arm's length and looks disgusted. And onto Goliath's severed head, I put my own features. (It is my face before the recent assault, Christ, I wouldn't want to frighten people too much.) The head hangs in darkness so that the black hair and beard framing the face blend off into the shadows, and there are four thin ropes of dark blood trailing down into space from the neck. And in one eye of the freshly severed head, there is still the faint glimmer of life.

That's me and that's the last painting I ever did.

Spectator, viewer, audience, however you care to call yourself; I address you here, with this, my final picture.

Cast a cold eye on it all, and on my work. I am still alive.

Post Scriptum

Word has reached me via the Marchesa that the Pope is considering a pardon. At long last, great news, the best I have had in years. I will set out for Rome, straightway, whether the pardon be confirmed or no. It is July and I will leave soon and take a boat to Civitavecchia, the port authority for Rome.

They will surely let me live while His Holiness thinks on the matter. Rome I know, Rome I can take care of myself in, Rome cannot hurt me for I swim in its currents and I know its tides which carry me along safe.

Did I tell you I had learned to swim in Sicily? Minitti taught me, on the shore at Selinunte. It was fun, though I cannot see the point of it.

I dream still of Fillide. Soon I shall see her again. And I worry about that. Perhaps she has aged. Grown fat perhaps. Gone grey, or acquired a moustache. Somehow I doubt it. I see her in my mind's eye exactly as she was, and while I can think of more conventionally beautiful women, yet none stirs my blood as the vision of my Fillide.

Memo from Bellarmino

To:

His Holiness Pope Paul V

From:

Cardinal Bellarmino, Chief Inquisitor, Society of Jesus.

Official memorandum.

MOST SECRET

Delivered Personally by Hand of Author

The initial stages of our plan worked well. The monk who was tending the painter would often hear his confessions and note them down and duly pass them back to us. They simply confirmed what we have always known about the stinking little atheist. The word was passed to the Marchesa da Caravaggio (who is no relation of the painter) of Your Holiness's consideration of a pardon, and while she expressed some doubts nonetheless she did believe it, since she knew that your relation Gonzaga was desirous of meeting the painter and acquiring some of his pictures.

No doubt that was the clinching matter, for the man

does love to paint, however blasphemously. Not even his recent wounds and long convalescence could keep him from working at full pressure.

I have prepared here a short account of Caravaggio's death, which we will give to the painter Baglione, who is one of our very own. He has done many worthy and holy paintings for the Jesuits and does not paint blasphemous rubbish like the man we have been speaking of. Baglione likes to write up the lives of his contemporaries and fellow painters and his accounts are published and circulate among the intelligentsia, so will one day come to be taken at their value and recorded in the *storia* of our age. It is not the truth, but it is acceptable, for that contemptible and blasphemous painter does not deserve the truth. God alone will know the truth and I am content to let the people believe he died a stupid, wasted death, unaided by God's grace. Thus perish all who would question the priesthood, and the authority of Your Holiness.

True, Baglione once sued Caravaggio for defamation and lost, so we must be scrupulous in his writing it up, in order that he look fair and unbiased toward the man, perhaps just dropping the occasional slight hint to show that he disliked him. For that would be natural to any man. But let Baglione bear no grudge in the writing, in order to suggest that he is a good and charitable Catholic, which I know him to be.

Here are the salient points of my account of Caravaggio's death, which I will pass on to Baglione:

> He set out in a boat with a few paintings to come to Rome, returning on the word of the Cardinal Gonzaga, who was negotiating his pardon with the Pope Paul V. When he arrived on the beach, he was arrested by mistake for someone else and put in prison, where he was held for two days and then released . . .

The captain of the garrison was under our instruction, Holiness, although he did not quite do as this report suggests.

Notice, Holiness, that the actual setting is vague. We will only suggest later in other reports that this place is Palo, just on the coast below Civitavecchia, where there is indeed a garrison, and is indeed where we intended Caravaggio to meet his fate. The report continues:

> He was held for two days and then released. The boat had disappeared. He flew into a rage and in desperation he started along the beach under the fierce July sun like a madman, trying to catch sight of the felucca that had his belongings.

Note, Holiness, the reference to his behaving like a madman. An acute touch I think, given his well-known behaviour and his *cervello straniero*, his strange brain. The sun too would play a part in his final 'fever'.

He finally came to a place where he was put to bed with a

raging fever. And so, with the aid of neither God nor man, in a few days he was dead, as wretchedly as he had lived.

The last phrase is an apt summation, I think, and we will put it about that he died at Porto Ercole, further up the coast, about seventy miles through malarial swamps, which would account for the madman's deathly fever. Porto Ercole is a Godforsaken spot, of no importance whatsoever, with only a small Spanish garrison and a little hospital for travellers. One death more or less there would not be noticed, and the local priest is a drunk and notoriously lax with his records. We might be able to sneak in an entry to his record of deaths, or we might just let it go, for no one would seek it out especially, nor question its absence. I would suggest, Holiness, that this message be stored in our most secret vault and not released until at least the next millennium.

It was in fact Palo where he was doomed.

The Last Stand

J'y suis, j'y reste.

Marshal MacMahon, when urged to abandon
the Malakoff tower. 1855

These may be the last words you will hear from me. Thank you for bearing with me so long. I know my memory is faulty, but the story was worth the candle, I think.

A felucca arrived at the quayside, and I could hear them loading it up. I know the cries of the sailors well, by now. From Rome, through Malta, Sicily and finally here at Naples, back on the mainland within reach of Rome, I have come to know ports and ships and their traffic only too well. The men who sail this inland sea are men like any other; the sort that I put in paintings as saints and martyrs and betrayers. Men like you.

A few, a very few, are even like me. I can spot them straight away, those few who carry the mark of Cain. They carry themselves in a different way, and stand apart from the rest. They don't say much, and don't mingle with other men. They don't joke much either, neither do they swear or blaspheme. When they look out to sea their brows knit, and their eyes narrow, and you can see that their gaze carries clear across to the far horizon, miles from where they stand at the rail. Who knows what they are thinking? They eat alone and that sparingly. I never saw a fat murderer. Me? I have always been as thin as a one of my hogs'-hair brushes. And they tell me that for the last four years I had a hunted look. Hah. Not any more. I am on my way. They won't get me now.

My felucca stopped at Palo, but the sailors did not warn me of it. It seems strange, for we had not reached Civitavecchia, which was but a few more miles up the coast. One sailor mumbled something about a change of plan and picking someone up, but did not sound at all convincing. I disembarked to stretch my legs and was immediately seized by a group of Spanish soldiers and frog-marched up to the fortress. Something fishy is going on, although they didn't seem especially agitated about me, just under the impression that I was wanted for something. Well, that could be true enough, God knows I have done enough to be wanted for a hundred crimes, though not lately. Something is afoot, and yet I cannot see what.

They held me overnight, although they treated me well and put me in a large furnished room, and fed me decent food, so that it was not like prison, more like a house arrest. And the next morning the captain saw me in his room, and talked with me, not unkindly, and verified who I was. He said that they were looking for another man called Polidoro da Caravaggio who is also known to be in these parts, and that he looks something like me. His soldiers had mistaken me for him. 'That is all,' he said, 'and you are free to go with my apologies.'

I stepped out into the morning sunlight, still puzzling on this story for it did not ring true at all. The soldiers had not been looking along the faces of those on board. They had just marched straight up to me and bundled me off. And if they are working in the pay of the Maltese or of the Vatican why not just finish me off overnight there and then? They could have used poison as they did with poor old Cardinal del Monte. Too many witnesses, I suppose. Too many saw me disembark, too many saw me taken in arrest, then more soldiers and officials and others at the castle.

And I walked back in the sunshine toward the beach and disaster then struck.

My felucca was already under sail and out to sea. I shouted and roared till I was hoarse, and waved my arms like a madman. But they were gone, and my goods with them. And I sank to my knees in my wretchedness and wept tears of hot rage, there into the sand. And when I raised my head I saw a man, standing at the stern of the boat, dressed in some finery and a feathered hat. He was not a sailor. He was staring at me, and I knew that they had not come by chance. He was taking my goods back to Rome to the Vatican bastards via Civitavecchia. The four paintings, which I had cut from their frames and carried with me on my travels, were travelling back to the Pope. He would soon unlock the secrets they contained.

So I got up and squared my shoulders back and walked a little way along the beach to compose myself and think. And presently I came to a small rocky bay, only a few hundred yards from the main part of Palo, but well hidden, with woods and dense thickets and undergrowth surrounding it.

They were waiting for me.

Caravaggio: My Last Words

So there it is, I have told you of my crimes. As I said, the only painting that I ever signed was a beheading of John the Baptist, and I wrote in the blood that flowed from his severed neck *Feci Michel M.* I, Caravaggio, did this.

It is not much, is it? Not in the general scheme of things. A few deaths of men that deserved to die. But I am not sorry for it. I am proud of what I did for it fed the rage in me, the rage that has governed all my life, and continues even now. I have seen men grovel and spew pathetic recrimi nations on themselves when their crimes are found out. They will hang their heads, and beg the Lord for mercy, and cry out that they must be punished. It is called jailhouse penitence, and I will have none of it. I am unrepentant. Better, I glory in what I did. It made me a god, and when I meet my end, which must be soon, I will outface whosoever I find when I cross over. He will understand.

The one – the only – thing I miss is my paintings. They were my children. The Pope will have them soon, and will be greedily reading the secret messages I encoded in them. For I was a spy too, for the French. I wish I had time to tell you all about that, for it was of passing interest.

CARAVAGGIO

Think what you like of me, I never cared for others' good opinion. My day is ended. Night is approaching and with it the dark.

But cast a cold eye on my paintings, look long and look hard, for there you will see the only things I ever cared about. And mark well this: I never painted 'beauty'. All I say is: 'This is here.'

A Secret Report of the Painter's Death

To:

His Holiness Paul V.

From:

Cardinal Bellarmino, Chief Inquisitor. Society of Jesus.

Official memorandum.

MOST SECRET

Delivered Personally.

To be destroyed by fire.

Our knights have returned from their mission and they have reported to me that he was killed in a small secluded bay, a little way up the coast from the beaching point at Palo. The knight who struck the killing blow was the Maltese who has been helping us track him and also helping train up our soldiers, who are not so battle-wise as theirs.

Alas four of their number were killed in the undertaking, by the painter, who was not only a skilled fighter, but inspired by the Devil.

CARAVAGGIO

At the very least we are all spared the horror of having to interrogate such a devil in the flesh, although I feel God's will coursing through my veins when I think of how I might have done it. The suffering of such a man would have pleased the Good Lord through me.

His body was sewn in a sack, weighted with stones and thrown into the sea. The filthy little dauber. So end all blasphemers.

The True Account of the Painter's Death

A Missive

To:

Alof de Wignacourt, Grand Master of the Knights of Malta.

From:

Your Brother Knight Don Rodriguez de la Sierra within the Spanish wing of the Order, charged with leading the Caravaggio mission with knights from the Vatican Secret Service.

Delivered by your most favoured messenger, your pageboy from within the French Wing of the Order.

Accept only from him.

Destroy by burning after reading.

We surrounded him and one of the Vatican guard went in first for I had been training him in feats of arms, and he was proud and wanted to please his masters and have the distinction of being the true executioner. Stupid boy. His reach exceeded his grasp. I had seen the painter in action but never before did I see him duel so well. After a few passes, he performed a manoeuvre I had never seen before.

It was a set of complicated thrusts, which I could follow with my eye quite easily although they both were very fast with a sword. Then the painter did his main business. He thrust a feint to the *octave*, followed by . . . the very briefest hesitation. And here was his true cunning, here was, I am moved to say, the beauty of the thing. The hesitation was entirely believable. He was like the very best kind of actor. His opponent, the Vatican boy, believed in that man's hesitation entirely. And then, the simplest move on the part of the painter, and yet, as I see it now and relive it all over in my mind's eye, with much relish I must admit, it has to be said that it is the only possible move. A counter-thrust over the arm to the *seconde*. That belief on the part of the Vatican boy in the painter's trick cost him his life.

The painter's blade went clean through the boy's neck, cut the artery, just so, without wrenching, and was out again in a trice, with blood spouting from the boy's neck like a double-pressured fountain. The boy fell to the sand, his hands grappling at his throat, already no more than a side of meat.

Christ, that struck home with the onlookers. That hit them where they lived, and gave the whole gang pause, I can tell you. For they are good men, but still unblooded. And the painter looked at each of us in turn.

I have never seen a man so unafraid. There he was, on

this rocky shore, surround by a half-circle of us five, with nothing at his back but the sea. And his hideous face was swelling and turning red, and his nostrils were opened like a horse, and he threw his head around to clear his long black hair from his eyes, and wiped his brow with one hand and shouted 'Hah!' at the top of his voice. And I tell you, even I was afraid. Not him, though.

Several of the Vatican boys raised their swords and made a brief sally toward him, but their heart wasn't in it, he could tell that as plainly as if he were reading a letter from them. He ran toward them and they skittered and backed. But slowly, very slowly, the circle was shortening its diameter, and closing in on him.

I was still confident of the outcome, yet even then a small seed of doubt was growing in my mind. Surely he could not kill us all?

Well, he did for three more, in the quickest flurry of action I have ever seen. He swung his cloak around at one, and just as the boy thrust through the cloak at the man, suddenly the man was not where he should have been. I do not know how he did it. And the boy's sword got tangled in the cloak. And that was the end of him.

Then the painter did the most extraordinary leap in the air, and took two others, one with his dagger, one with his sword, almost simultaneously. Still, we were closing in, and I could see he was wounded on an arm, and his face had opened up across a cheek and was bleeding badly. He must have been nearly forty years of age, yet he had the grace and spring and rage of a tiger.

And still we closed further in. And, well, I commended my soul to the Lord, for I knew if ever we were to succeed, then I must do the deed. But I tell you, he was my equal at the least, and I knew it would not an easy thing.

And then he was backed up onto a small spit of rock, jutting out slightly into the bay, with the sea bursting up occasionally through a little funnel in the rock, and making a small fountain of spray. I remember noticing that shattering little rainbow of water quite distinctly, for as it happened, he turned, clasped his hands ahead of him as if in prayer and dived into the water.

We went to the edge, and watched, and it was a long while before he surfaced, quite a way out into the bay. And his head was within the shadow of a large tree on the other side of the bay, which was cast across the water by the morning sun. And we watched some more, as he submerged again, and after that we never saw anything of him again.

We none of us could swim.

The Vatican boys got nervous. So I swore them to secrecy, and we reported back to Cardinal Bellarmino, that stinking little torturer, that we had killed the man as ordered, put him in a sack and slung him out to sea. 'Praise be to God,' he said. 'So perish all blasphemers.'

'Amen,' we said, looking all long-faced and holy. And then we went to wash away the bad taste from our mouths with wine. We drank all night, but none of us could get drunk.

Well, there it is. He was wounded and like as not to drown or bleed to death. We never saw him again, not that day nor the next, in spite of us trawling up and down the coast in hope of some sighting.

But I tell you this. I hope he escaped.

I have looked at his paintings, though they mean little to me, for I am not a man much taken with art. I have followed him around. I have watched while he whored and gambled and drank. I have watched while he ran rings around my men, and even watched while he killed a few.

I know of his crimes and I know why he needed to be silenced. But he was a prince among fighters. And that is something I know a little about.

Perhaps he will resurface some day, elsewhere. God keep him wherever he may be, here, above or below. For there is one thing I have come to know of him, and it was this. They say his dagger was inscribed thus: *Nec Spe. Nec Metu.* No hope. No fear.

But if he ever had a motto it was surely this.

Life and nothing but.

Finis